Around and around and around it goes . . .

A baseball cap came flying through the air. The carousel was going faster and faster. I saw a woman's pocketbook get pulled off her arm by the centrifugal force created by the wild ride. Popcorn flew through the air, yanked out of the tubs the kids on the merry-go-round were holding.

The carousel spun even faster. The tinkly music started to sound warped as the ride whooshed by.

"Look out!" Joe yelled as a camcorder came flying toward me. I ducked just in time.

"Somebody stop that thing!" a nearby father shouted. His face was white with fear.

UNDERCOVER BROTHERS™

#1 *Extreme Danger*
#2 *Running on Fumes*
#3 *Boardwalk Bust*
#4 *Thrill Ride*

Available from Simon & Schuster

THE HARDY BOYS

UNDERCOVER BROTHERS™

#4   ## Thrill Ride

FRANKLIN W. DIXON

Aladdin Paperbacks

New York   London   Toronto   Sydney

This book is a work of fiction. Any references to historical events, real people, or real locales are used fictitiously. Other names, characters, places, and incidents are the product of the author's imagination, and any resemblance to actual events or locales or persons, living or dead, is entirely coincidental.

❧ ALADDIN PAPERBACKS
An imprint of Simon & Schuster
Children's Publishing Division
1230 Avenue of the Americas
New York, NY 10020

Copyright © 2005 by Simon & Schuster, Inc.

All rights reserved, including the right of
reproduction in whole or in part in any form.
THE HARDY BOYS MYSTERY STORIES and HARDY BOYS
UNDERCOVER BROTHERS are trademarks of Simon & Schuster, Inc.
ALADDIN PAPERBACKS and colophon are trademarks of
Simon & Schuster, Inc.
Designed by Lisa Vega
The text of this book was set in Aldine 401BT.
Manufactured in the United States of America
First Aladdin Paperbacks edition June 2005
20 19 18 17 16 15 14 13

Library of Congress Control Number: 2004117445
ISBN-13: 978-1-4169-0005-4
ISBN-10: 1-4169-0005-5

TABLE OF CONTENTS

1.	*Rumble!*	1
2.	*Special Delivery*	13
3.	*Doom Rider*	23
4.	*An Explosive Discovery*	40
5.	*The Real Target?*	57
6.	*Not-So-Merry-Go-Round*	69
7.	*Innocent Bystander*	80
8.	*Rotten Meat*	89
9.	*Down the Wormhole*	97
10.	*Working Out*	114
11.	*Hall of Horror*	125
12.	*Zombie!*	133
13.	*In the Dungeon*	141
14.	*Mission Accomplished*	149

1.

RUMBLE!

"He's always come through for us and he will now!" Riff yelled.

A burst of music rang through the air.

Onstage, one of the big musical numbers in the summer stock production of *West Side Story* was just about to begin. Backstage, my brother Frank had just been stabbed in the stomach.

"Frank!" I cried, trying to keep my voice down.

With all the actors either onstage or in one of the dressing rooms upstairs—and the stage manager nowhere to be found—it was just Frank and me against DJ and Big T, two of the nastiest lowlifes I'd ever met.

Frank and I had been sent to investigate a drag-racing ring. We'd never expected it to lead us to a theater with a play in mid-performance! DJ and Big T were two of the main criminals in the racing ring. They stole from anyone and anything to finance their expensive automotive habit.

DJ stood over Frank, who slumped on the floor holding his stomach. His mouth was open in a silent O of pain and disbelief.

Like most brothers, Frank and I have our differences. He's got no sense of humor; I've got a great one. He spends way too much time looking things up on the Internet library reference sites; I spend way too much time playing games on my Xbox. And most recently, that mysterious attraction he holds for girls made it impossible for me to get noticed by Angela Mendes.

But I really didn't want him to get stabbed. Not even a little. I could barely believe my eyes. I mean, we've escaped a million life-threatening situations on our missions for American Teens Against Crime, or ATAC for short. How could Frank get stabbed by some degenerate at the Croton-on-Hudson Theater? These losers were trying to steal the box office money the summer stock company was raising for the When Wishes Come True Foundation.

Guys like that shouldn't be able to stab my brother.

DJ—a small, wiry creep with long greasy hair

and an even greasier smile—glanced at me over Frank's crumpled body. DJ had the chipped teeth of a fighter. He grabbed the metal lockbox the money was in and headed for the exit.

But the only way out was onto the stage.

DJ yanked aside the curtain—only to find twenty or thirty fake gang members dancing across the stage.

I shook my head, trying to clear it. Right after Frank took the knife, everything seemed to slow down to molasses pace, like someone hit the SLOW button on a remote.

I had to get to Frank. But I'd been in the middle of a fight. I turned to face Big T, a beefy guy with cropped hair and the typical tough-guy tattoo around his bicep.

I'd meant to turn back to Big T. Instead, I turned back to his fist.

Coming right at me.

And someone had hit the PLAY button again, because his fist was coming in *fast.*

I've taken a lot of punches on my ATAC missions, and I know that big guys usually throw these roundhouse punches. All the way around their bodies, leading with their shoulder. No matter how fast they move, there is always time to step toward them and get inside the arc of their fist.

So that's what I did.

3

As fast as possible, I moved close to Big T to get my head out of the way. Then I bent my knees and sidestepped out of range.

I had to get to Frank, who was still lying on the floor. And making a weird gesture with his hand.

What was he doing?

He pointed up and then at the wall. Then he did it again.

Maybe he was just in so much pain that he was having spasms.

DJ decided not to run out on stage. I guess disrupting the show in front of a packed audience would call too much attention to him and Big T. He whirled away from the curtain and took off for the ladder leading to the catwalk that ran across the top of the stage. I started after him.

But I couldn't move. Big T had grabbed the back of my jacket.

No problem. I wriggled out of it and took a few steps toward Frank.

He kept making those weird gestures. And his eyes were unmistakably saying, "Pay attention, bonehead."

Then I got it. He was signaling me.

See, as I mentioned before, I had a thing for Angela, the actress who was playing Maria in *West Side Story*. She was totally gorgeous, and she was

4

only in town for the summer. So I had come to more rehearsals than I could count. I knew all the words to all the songs, all the steps to all the dances, and all the props and sets that moved on and off the stage. And so did Frank. Because the only way I could get Angela to come over and talk to me was to bring Frank with me. He's like a force of nature—girls love him. The problem is, he's so shy with them that he turns into a big dork when they're around. But for some reason they all like him. Including Angela.

Frank and I were there the day the summer stock director—in a fit of his self-proclaimed genius—got his carpentry team to rig up a special effect for the play. At just the right time in "When You're a Jet," the gang leader Riff kicks a trash can for emphasis. The can is supposed to fly off the stage—and I mean *fly*.

To get this effect, the can was connected by a nylon fishing wire threaded through a pulley system to a heavy sandbag. When the stage manager got the right cue, he'd make the sandbag drop to the floor backstage, pulling the trash can up and through the air.

I glanced up. The sandbag dangled ten feet above and just a few feet to the right of Big T's gigantic melon of a head.

I looked back at Frank. He was still lying on the ground, but he was close to the rope that needed to be untied to trigger the bag. So I turned on Big T with my fiercest look.

He laughed at me.

All I had to do was get him to step under the bag. I knew I couldn't get close to him. He was too big and too dangerous. And I knew he wasn't afraid of me, so he wouldn't run. But I also knew that Big T was not too bright—we're talking ten-, maybe twenty-watt bulb here. All I had to do was let him think he was going to win.

So I let him come to me. I sidestepped so he had to move under the bag.

The entire time I listened for the cue from the stage. No sense in ruining the show just because we were having a fight. The actor playing Riff was supposed to say, "I'm only gonna challenge him," and then kick the can. That was the cue for the sandbag to drop.

Frank was gesturing frantically for me to get Big T under the bag. But Angela would be so upset if the show got ruined by a special effect going off at the wrong time.

I needed to wait for just a few more lines, so I circled again. Big T continued to follow me, stepping after me as if connected by a leash.

There!

Frank scrambled up to his feet. Big T stopped, surprised that Frank was moving so fast. Come to think of it, so was I. But I had no more time to wonder about it because . . .

"I'm only gonna challenge him," Riff sneered. He kicked the can.

Frank released the rope.

Wham!

The sandbag came down on cue—right on Big T's head. No one on stage or in the audience was any the wiser. And certainly Big T wouldn't be either. He was out cold on the floor.

I ran over to Frank.

"Are you okay?" I whispered, reaching to steady him. But he didn't need my help.

"I'm fine, Joe." He handed me the gleaming knife. "It's one of the stage knives. Retractable blades."

I pressed the point of the knife against the upturned palm of my hand. Sure enough, it slid back into the handle like it was supposed to.

"I pulled it on that loser and let him think he took it from me." Frank shook his hand in the air, sending tiny droplets of blood flying. "I cut myself on his stupid ring, though."

"It's a good thing Big T isn't the sharpest knife

in the drawer." I stabbed Frank in the shoulder with the fake blade. He didn't think my joke was funny. He never thinks my jokes are funny. Of course, I didn't think his pretending to be stabbed in the stomach was funny either.

Frank pointed at DJ, who was climbing down from the catwalk on the other side of the stage right now. With the metal cash box in one hand, the ladder was slow going, but he was still getting away. With all the money.

"We have to go after him." Frank started toward the ladder.

But I knew it was hopeless. We didn't have time to get all the way across the length of the stage. It would take too long to maneuver through all the props and sets stored backstage.

Luckily, I had a Plan B.

"Hey, Frank, can I have this dance?" I pointed at the stage.

"What?"

The Jets were just going into another of the director's bright ideas. The gang members start on our side of the stage and do this weird step-step-raise-your-knee-snap-with-your-arms-by-your-sides thing a few times across the stage. They looked like idiots every time they did it. But it got them across the stage pretty fast. We grabbed a couple of extra period hats and ran to the back of the line.

Suddenly we were out in the bright lights with the actors. Being onstage wasn't what I expected. You can barely see the audience at all. Just the first few rows and then darkness. It was a little like being alone, with just the other performers.

Except that off to the side of the first row, peering in from one of the exit doors, was Angela! Oh, man. Was she there to watch the scenes she wasn't in?

Well, not anymore. Now she was watching Frank. And so was I.

He stepped. Then stepped again. Then raised his knee—and saw Angela looking right at him.

Uh-oh, I thought.

My pumpkinhead of a brother stopped. Right there in the middle of the stage. He stood frozen, blushing from head to toe. I rolled my eyes. Frank can do anything except deal with cute girls.

I sped over to his side and poked him in the ribs.

Frank jumped back into action. We skipped the snap and just ran with our arms by our sides. We stayed behind the rest of the guys and caught up by the time we started stepping again.

Once we hit the other side, we ducked offstage, with no one the wiser. Well, except Angela, that is, and probably some of the guys onstage. But the show must go on, right?

We ran back into the darkness just as DJ was getting to the bottom of the ladder. It took a few seconds for our eyes to adjust after the bright lights of the stage. When they did, I saw DJ trying to get *his* eyes to adjust—to the fact that Frank was up and around instead of lying there with a knife in his stomach.

DJ ran toward the back exit, with Frank and me in hot pursuit. "We can't let him get out the door," I cried in a stage whisper.

If DJ got through that door, he'd be able to get to his hot rod. Our awesome, state-of-the-art motorcycles could catch his car, no problem. Only our bikes were in the front parking lot, all the way around the building.

If he got out the door, we'd lose him. And the money for the When Wishes Come True kids.

And we couldn't yell out for help, because then the show would come to a screeching halt and people might want their money back.

Besides, Frank and I always catch the bad guy. We've never been on a mission we couldn't handle.

Then I remembered. The stage manager had told me they stored tall scenery pieces under the stage. They lowered them down through a long trapdoor in the stage—three feet wide by fifteen feet long.

The crank to open the trapdoor was on this side of the stage.

"Make sure he doesn't get past that yellow painted area," I told Frank. He'd been so busy stammering and trying to avoid Angela whenever we were here that he'd never heard about the trapdoor. "And you stay out of it."

Frank nodded.

I ran to the side wall, where the crank was hidden behind the spiral staircase that led up to the dressing rooms. I'd have to do this quickly and just like the stage manager had showed me. There was some trick to get the crank going.

Too bad I couldn't remember what it was.

DJ ran into the yellow area, approaching the door. He glanced over his shoulder.

Frank threw the knife at him.

DJ dodged sideways—and stayed in the yellow area.

"DJ," Frank said—loud enough to hear, but quiet enough not to disturb the play. "How dumb are you? It's a fake knife."

The taunt stopped DJ just long enough for my brain to kick into gear. I remembered the trick. I wedged myself on the other side of the crank, with my back to the wall next to it, and put my left leg onto the handle. I pushed with all my strength.

The trapdoor opened.

And DJ disappeared as the floor vanished from underneath him.

Well, almost. At the last second he grabbed onto the edge of the floor.

He held on, dangling. And it was a long drop. Frank leaned over. "Here. Take my hand."

DJ looked at Frank's hand, then at the money box he'd have to drop if he did. His indecision cost him. His hand slipped and down he fell.

I knew he'd be okay, but it was going to leave a mark.

I walked up next to Frank. "Greed is a heavy burden," I joked.

Frank just looked at me and shook his head.

2.

SPECIAL DELIVERY

"And just where have you two been all day?" Aunt Trudy greeted us as we walked through the front door.

I shot a look at Joe. His clothes were still covered in dirt from the fight backstage. I quickly stuck my scraped-up hand in the pocket of my jeans. "We were at the theater," I said.

"The *theater*?" Mom sounded skeptical.

"Yeah. There was a summer stock production of *West Side Story*."

Now even Dad looked skeptical. We'd never told him we'd been hanging out at the summer stock theater lately. Joe had been too embarrassed about the theater part of it. I'd been too embarrassed about Angela having a crush on me. "The girl who stars in it is incredibly hot," Joe put in.

Mom and Aunt Trudy exchanged a smile, and Mom shook her head.

"Nice save," I murmured to Joe. I'm such an idiot around girls that I avoid them as much as I can. But Joe is always flirting with someone—and he'd spent half the summer flirting with Angela. Aunt Trudy and Mom would totally believe that he went to a play just to score points with a girl.

Dad was still studying the grime on Joe's shirt. He frowned. Dad's the only one who knows that we work for American Teens Against Crime—ATAC. Even though he cofounded the organization, he still worries about us when we're on missions. Obviously he could tell we'd been in a fight.

"How was it?" he asked. Mom probably thought he was asking about the play. But I knew he really wanted to know about our mission.

"It was great," I told him. "Not a single hitch."

"Sounds like your girl is a good actor in addition to her incredible hotness," Mom teased Joe.

"You should have put on a clean shirt if you wanted to impress her," Aunt Trudy added. "You look like you've been rolling in a pigsty. I expect you to wash up before dinner—and that is in exactly ten minutes."

"Pigs! Pigs! Pigs!" my pet parrot, Playback,

squawked from his perch on the back of Dad's chair.

Mom squinted at Joe's filthy shirt. He shot me a panicked look. Our mom's no fool—she works as a research librarian. It's not easy to keep her from finding out about our missions. And if she got a closer look at Joe's shirt, we'd be busted for sure!

The doorbell rang.

"Saved by the bell," Joe said. He rushed over and pulled open the front door.

"Pizza delivery!" The teenage guy on the porch wore an idiotic red-and-white uniform with a big red scarf tied around his neck. He held up two pizza boxes. "Two cheese pies," he announced with an Indian accent.

"All right!" Joe cried. "Nice going, Aunt Trudy."

Aunt Trudy frowned so hard I thought her face might crack. "I didn't order pizza. I made a big chef's salad."

"Oh." Joe turned away from the door, bummed.

"Sorry," I said to the pizza guy. "Looks like there was a mistake."

He shrugged. "Well, you can have the pies anyway. If I brought them back, they would just get cold."

"Really?" I asked. "Cool."

"Cool?" Aunt Trudy repeated. "You think a meal

filled with enough cholesterol, saturated fat, and sodium to choke a horse is *cool*?"

"Saturated fat!" squawked Playback. "Cool!"

"Actually, if these are plain cheese pies, they're not so bad," Mom put in. "The extremely high levels of saturated fat and sodium are usually found in pizza that contains meat—you know, a sausage or pepperoni pie. A plain cheese is fine." She winked at me. "As long as you don't eat it every day."

"Well, I think we should leave the pizza to the boys," Dad said, standing up. "Us old folks can dig into that salad." He ushered Mom and Aunt Trudy toward the kitchen.

That was weird. Dad loves pizza. Why would he want to let Joe and me have it all?

I turned back to the guy at the door. He was watching our parents leave the room. As soon as the kitchen door swung closed behind them, his whole expression changed. With one hand, he pulled the dumb red scarf off his neck.

"You're not really a delivery guy, are you?" I asked.

"Nope. I'm from ATAC," he replied. "My name is Vijay Patel."

"What are you talking about?" I said, playing dumb. ATAC is a secret organization. This kid could be trying to get us to spill information about our work—and we had no way of knowing who he really worked for.

"Oh. Sorry." Vijay bent down and put the pizza boxes on the doormat. He stuck out his hand to shake.

I grabbed on and did two hard up-and-down shakes followed by a wrist-grab, then a fist-touch, and finally one last up-and-down shake. "Okay, Vijay, you know the handshake," I said. "So you must really work for ATAC."

"Yes. I'm still a trainee. In fact, you two are the first real ATAC agents I've met." Vijay looked embarrassed. "I almost forgot that I had to identify myself with the secret handshake."

"No problem," Joe said. "We just have to be careful. Sometimes people set traps for us."

"I know," Vijay told us. "I've read about a lot of your cases in the ATAC files. You're two of our top agents!"

"Thanks," Joe said with a big grin. "It's nice to have a fan. How long have you been with the organization?"

"For a year," Vijay said. "I used to solve crimes in my neighborhood in Calcutta when I was little. I've always wanted to be a crime fighter."

"How long have you been in the United States?" I asked.

"My family moved here from India when I was twelve," Vijay said.

I heard the sound of plates clanking in the kitchen. We had to finish up with Vijay before Mom decided to come back out. "I guess our father recognized you as a fellow ATAC-er," I said. "Are you here on official business?"

"Yes." Vijay bent and opened the top pizza box. Inside was a video game disk. The title on the game read, THRILL RIDE.

Vijay handed me the disk, while Joe groaned in disappointment. "That's not real pizza?" he complained.

"No, but this is." Vijay picked up the second pizza box and gave it to Joe. "The folks at ATAC knew you'd be hungry after your last mission!"

"They're a class operation," Joe said happily. He's easy to please.

"There's one more thing," Vijay added. He pulled a tiny metal square from the pocket of his uniform. "We just used these in my last training session. I thought you guys might like one—it could come in handy."

"What is it?" I asked, taking the little silver box. "Some kind of cell phone?"

"No, it's a pocket strobe," Vijay explained. "Push

this button on the side, and the box will emit a flash of powerful light. But only for a second."

"So it's like a camera flash?" Joe asked.

"If it's a strobe light, it's much more powerful than a camera flash," I said.

"Yeah, it's really bright," Vijay agreed. "But you never know when you need some light."

"Cool. Thanks, Vijay," I said.

He tucked the now-empty pizza box under his arm and gave us both the secret handshake again. "I can't wait to tell the other trainees I met Frank and Joe Hardy," he said. "You guys are legends."

"Legends," Joe repeated as I closed the door behind Vijay. "I like the sound of that."

"Don't get so full of yourself that you forget we have a new mission," I told him. "Let's go pop this disk in the system."

Upstairs in my room, Joe dug into the pizza while I stuck "Thrill Ride" into my gaming system.

A video of a roller coaster came onto the TV screen. People screamed as they turned upside down on a wicked coaster loop. Another rockin' coaster followed; then another.

"I like this mission already," Joe mumbled through a mouthful of pizza.

"Amusement park rides are built to thrill," a

deep voice said over the coaster montage. "Gravity-defying turns and deadly dangerous drops. But it's all fun and games. Isn't it?"

The image zoomed in on the screaming face of a young guy, swooping straight into his mouth, open in a yell of terror, and ending in blackness.

"Uh-oh," I murmured. I had a feeling this mission *wasn't* going to be fun and games.

The blackness turned gray, then lightened to a black-and-white still photo of an old amusement park on a paved lot. Judging from the grainy photo and the strange clothes the people wore, this picture had been taken at least seventy or eighty years ago.

"Uncle Bernie's Fun Park," the deep voice announced. "Amusing and delighting the people of Holyoke, Massachusetts, since 1924."

The picture faded out and was replaced by a photo of a middle-aged woman smiling sweetly at the camera.

"Maggie Soto," the voice said. "Age forty-five, a schoolteacher and a mother of two. She was killed last week at Uncle Bernie's Fun Park."

I heard Joe gasp. I put down the slice I'd been eating. Pizza didn't seem so good all of a sudden. What had happened to this woman?

As if he could read my mind, the announcer

explained, "Maggie was riding on the Doom Rider roller coaster when the ride malfunctioned."

Maggie's smiling face vanished and was replaced by a picture of the coaster. It looked just like any other medium-sized roller coaster. No loops, but a lot of big drops and a few tunnels.

"In the second tunnel, a large piece of interior scenery broke off the ceiling," the announcer said. "The collapse happened immediately above Maggie's car. It injured her spine, and she died a few hours later."

"Aren't roller coasters inspected for safety like every day?" Joe asked.

"Uncle Bernie's Fun Park is maintaining that Maggie's death was an accident," the announcer said. "Their safety inspections are up-to-date, safety inspectors found nothing wrong with the coaster tracks or the cart she was riding in, and the local police have determined that no one had a motive to harm Maggie Soto."

"So what's our mission?" I asked. Sometimes the mission disks are so detailed that it almost seems like they're interactive.

Sure enough, the announcer answered as if he'd heard me.

"Your mission is to check out the amusement park," he said. "We here at ATAC are not convinced that this incident was an accident. We suspect that there may have been foul play, and you boys have to find out for sure."

I shot a look at Joe. "Before something else happens," I said.

"Before someone else gets hurt," the announcer finished. "This mission, like every mission, is top secret. In five seconds this disk will be reformatted into a regular CD."

Five seconds later, an old Aerosmith song blasted out of the TV speakers. But I was still thinking about Maggie Soto. What had really happened on that ride?

3.

DOOM RIDER

"You boys be careful," Dad said early the next morning.

I was tempted to roll my eyes, but I held back. Dad says that every time we leave for a mission. You'd think he was a regular father, the way he worries. Not Fenton Hardy, ex-cop and cofounder of the coolest crime-fighting organization ever. Dad was the one who recruited Frank and me to the ATAC team, but I guess that doesn't stop him from worrying about us.

"I'm still allowed to be concerned for your safety," Dad said. "Okay, Joe?"

"Yeah," I agreed. Obviously he knew what I was thinking even if I didn't roll my eyes. That's because he's such a great investigator—he can read people's body language.

Frank was still putting on his motorcycle helmet, but I was geared up and ready to go. I couldn't wait to get on the road. Sitting on my tricked-out cycle in the driveway was no fun at all.

"We'll be careful," Frank assured our father. "Are you going to tell Mom where we're going?"

"I'll say you went to an amusement park," Dad said. "I just won't say why."

"Sounds good. See you later." I revved up my bike, and Frank and I took off. In the sideview, I could see Dad standing in front of the house, watching us go.

The truth is, I feel better knowing he's got our backs. But I would never tell him that.

It took us almost four hours to get to Holyoke, Massachusetts. But four hours on the bike feels like no time. I could ride that thing all day!

We pulled into the parking lot of Uncle Bernie's Fun Park. The photo on the mission disk had been really old, but the amusement park still looked exactly the same. The lot was paved with old white concrete, grass grew up between the cracks, and the boards that made up the welcome sign looked like they were ready to collapse into sawdust.

"They haven't updated this place much," Frank commented.

"Not since the Dark Ages," I agreed. In fact, the only thing about the park that looked new—well, post-1970, anyway—was the roller coaster. It rose above the park, all gleaming metal and black paint. The way it loomed over the rinky-dink rides from the 1920s made the coaster look like some kind of monster.

"Let's go," Frank said.

I hopped off my bike and headed for the ticket booth. It was an old-fashioned wooden one that looked like a phone booth. "This is the best mission ever," I said. "Can you believe we've been *assigned* to go on amusement park rides?" Even if Uncle Bernie's was an old park, it would still be cool to go on the bumper cars and the slide.

"Don't get too excited," Frank warned. "Remember, that poor lady died here last week. And she may have been murdered."

That's my brother, always a downer. "I know," I said. "And I intend to find out what really happened." I couldn't get Maggie Soto's face out of my mind. If she'd been a victim of foul play, I wouldn't rest until her killer was behind bars.

"Let's check out the place first, get a feel for who

works here," Frank suggested. He paid for two admissions to the park and led the way inside.

The first attraction we came to was a flume ride. The cars were cool because they looked like real logs that had been carved into little canoes. But the water was only a foot deep and there were no big drops. I like a flume ride that dumps you fifty feet and creates a humongous splash. Still, the flume was packed with people, and the line had to be a half-hour wait. It was pretty hot out—I guess people like to get into whatever water they can find.

"Look at the girl running the ride," I said to Frank. She was about our age, with long dark hair pulled into two braids. That might have looked dorky on some girls, but she was gorgeous. On her the braids looked flirty and a little punk.

"She doesn't seem very suspicious," Frank said. "She just looks bored."

The girl yawned as she pushed the button to start the next log flume on its way down the fake river.

"I didn't think she was suspicious. Just hot," I informed my brother. He's so dense when it comes to girls.

"I think we should talk to that guy," Frank said. He nodded toward a gangly looking man dressed

26

in a blue-and-white striped suit. The dude was seriously tall. He must've been at least eight feet. He towered over the crowd as he walked forward. And there was something weird about his gait. There could only be one explanation: He was walking on stilts.

As the crowd cleared in front of him, I could see that I was right—the bottom half of his wide striped pants fluttered in the breeze as he walked. The stilts underneath were connected to his super-big shoes.

"Hey!" Frank called up to the guy. "You're pretty good at that. How long have you been stilt-walking?"

The guy peered down at us as if he was surprised that anyone was talking to him. I guess he didn't get much conversation way up there.

"Too long," he said. "I've been working at Uncle Bernie's for twelve summers now. This is my last one."

"How come?" I asked.

The guy pulled off his straw hat and mopped his brow. "Twelve years, no raise," he said. "I'm sick of it. Next summer I'm gonna find some other place to work. I could make more money with a traveling carnival." He slapped the hat back on his head and stomped off through the crowded park.

"O-kay," I said. "He's not too happy here. You think that makes him a suspect?"

Frank shrugged. "We don't even know if there was a crime yet. I don't think we can start calling people suspects."

"Check out the haunted house," I said. "I love haunted houses."

"That one looks pretty lame," Frank replied. "The back door is even open."

Sure enough, one of the employee-access doors to the house stood open. The outside of the door was painted to look like a column that was part of the mansion, complete with a spiderweb stretched over the top. But with the door open, the whole illusion was ruined. We could see right into the darkness inside and hear the screams of the people within.

As I watched, an elderly man in a faded blue jumpsuit came out of the haunted house. He was pushing a bucket with a mop sticking out of it. He let the door slam behind him without even caring about the noise it made.

"I'd like to talk to him," I said, following the old guy.

We caught up to him in a tin maintenance shed behind the kiddie swing ride. "Excuse me," I called.

The old guy turned around. "Whaddya want?" he growled.

"Uh . . . are you the janitor here?" I asked.

"Not anymore," he said. "Now I'm called the maintenance coordinator." He rolled his eyes.

"Why?" Frank asked.

"Because I asked old Bernie for a raise," the man said. "So he gave me a new job title instead."

"A new job title but no money?" I said. "That doesn't seem fair."

"Tell me about it. Bernie expected me to be thrilled. Seemed to think a new title would raise my self-esteem." He broke into a dry laugh that sounded more like a cough. "I don't care about self-esteem. I just wanted to make more than minimum wage."

"How long have you been working for Uncle Bernie?" Frank asked.

The man squinted at him suspiciously. "Why are you kids so curious?" he asked.

"We were thinking of applying for jobs here," I said, thinking fast. "We figured we'd ask what kind of employer Uncle Bernie was."

"He's the worst employer in Massachusetts," the man said. "Stingy and mean. Why, when that lady died on the coaster last week, all Bernie cared about was the bad publicity. He didn't even call her family to say he was sorry."

"Wow," Frank said. "Were you here when it happened?"

"Of course," the maintenance man said. "I'm always here. You think old Bernie gives us any time off?"

"Did you see the accident?" I asked. "Do you know how it happened?"

"Nah. I was clear across the park, cleaning up a milkshake that spilled on the teacup ride." The man turned to go inside the shed. "My advice to you boys is to get a job somewhere else. Anywhere else." He shut the door behind him.

"One thing's clear. Uncle Bernie isn't very popular," Frank said.

"But that still doesn't help us figure out what happened to Maggie Soto," I said.

"Let's head over to the roller coaster," Frank suggested. "We need to look at the scene of the crime . . . or the accident."

"Right." I glanced up. It wasn't hard to spot the coaster—the thing was the biggest ride in the park. You could see it from everywhere. I led the way toward it, past the game booths and around the carousel.

"Hang on," Frank said. "I need a drink after that long drive up here." He got in line at an old-fashioned concession cart on wheels. A pretty Asian girl manned the cart while a big, muscular bald guy stood nearby. He was obviously the one who pushed the cart from place to place. One entire arm was covered in tattoos, while the other just had one, a picture of a cat with the name LULU underneath.

"Hi. Two Cokes, please," Frank told the girl when it was his turn.

"Sure." She reached into the portable ice chest to get them.

"Hot out today, huh?" I said, flirting. "I hope you get a break soon."

The muscular guy snorted. "Yeah, right," he said. "We don't even know what a break is."

"Come on, Jonesy, it's not that bad," the girl replied. "We get time off for lunch."

"Ten minutes. Barely enough time to down a burger," Jonesy muttered.

Frank frowned. "You get only one ten-minute break a day? That's illegal."

Jonesy shrugged. "Tell it to old Bernie. He only cares about the law when they're here to investigate."

The girl made a face. "It's true. When the cops were here last week, all of a sudden we got an hour for lunch and ten-minute breaks twice a day. Once their investigation was over, it was back to no breaks at all."

"How long were the cops here?" Frank asked.

"Two days," the girl said. "They had the whole roller coaster roped off."

"It must've been a shock to have a death here," I said. "You guys must've been really upset."

"Just upset that it wasn't old Bernie who got killed on the coaster," Jonesy said. He smiled, revealing sharp gold teeth where his canines should be.

The girl shook her head. "Don't mind Jonesy," she told me. "He's always cranky."

"What about you?" I asked. "Do you like working here?"

"Not really." She gave me a big smile. "But I like it when there are cute customers to talk to."

I opened my mouth to flirt back . . . and that's when I realized that she was now gazing at Frank. *Smiling* at Frank. She'd forgotten I was even there.

What *is* it with him and girls?

"Can we get some service, please?" snapped a woman behind us. She had three little kids pulling on her arms.

"Sorry," I said, stepping aside. Frank grabbed the Cokes and followed me.

"What do you think about that big guy?" he said. "Sounded like he really wants to do Bernie in."

"You think maybe he tampered with the roller coaster?" I asked.

"Maybe," Frank said. "We'd better make sure the

SUSPECT PROFILE

Name: Samuel "Jonesy" Jones

Hometown: Albuquerque, New Mexico

Physical description: Age 29, 6'2", 250 lbs. Bald. Tattoo of his childhood pet, Lulu, on left arm.

Occupation: Concession worker at Uncle Bernie's Fun Park

Background: Child of divorce. Grew up in a run-down section of town.

Suspicious behavior: Heard to say that he wished Uncle Bernie harm.

Suspected of: Tampering with the roller coaster.

Possible motives: Revenge against Uncle Bernie's unfair treatment of his workers.

roller coaster was tampered with before we jump to conclusions."

We downed the sodas on the way to the coaster. I was surprised there wasn't a line wrapped all the way around the ride—usually roller coasters are the most popular rides at amusement parks.

"I bet people are staying away because they're freaked out by the accident last week," I said.

"Nope." Frank pointed to the front entrance of the coaster. "The ride's just closed."

I stared at the big black-metal gateway to the coaster. A neon sign read "Doom Rider." The words blinked on and off in an electric blue color. But a chain over the entrance made it clear that no one was allowed on.

"No way," I groaned. "If the cops are done investigating, why is it closed?"

Frank went closer to the chain. There was a small sign attached to it. "'Closed for repair work,'" he read aloud. "Looks like we can't get in this way."

"Then we'll have to find another way in," I said.

Frank nodded. We walked casually along the fence that surrounded the Doom Rider, looking for a back way in. But the fence went all the way around the coaster without a single break.

"What do we do now?" I asked.

"There has to be some kind of employee access," Frank replied. "And there should also be an emergency exit."

I glanced around. The coaster was all the way at the end of the amusement park—you had to walk past all the other rides and games to get to the Doom Rider. Since it was closed, there weren't many people around today. Just the lonely roller coaster and a few tin sheds.

"That's it!" I cried.

"What is?" Frank asked.

I gestured to the tin sheds. One of them had a KEEP OUT sign on the door.

"I'm guessing that's the emergency exit from the Doom Rider," I said. "This old pavement isn't strong enough to support the weight of the coaster. There has to be newer concrete underneath. And probably a control room or something."

"Good thinking," Frank said.

We went over to the door. I kept a lookout while Frank picked the lock on the doorknob. We always bring our lock picks with us on missions.

"We're in," he told me. We slipped through the door.

Just as I'd expected, the door led into a stairway that plunged under the ground. We hurried down and found ourselves in a storage room built of concrete underneath the old paved-over land. On one side was a mess of electronics. That had to be the control system for the coaster.

"It's like a garage," Frank said. "There are coaster parts all over the place."

"Yeah, but we're here to check out the ride, not the parts," I said. "Look!"

In the center of the room, a ladder led up to a trapdoor in the ceiling. That had to be where the storage room connected to the actual roller coaster.

We climbed up and made our way through to the coaster. Without the cars going, the whole thing just looked like a series of ladders and train tracks that criss-crossed every so often. "What are we looking for?" I asked Frank. "The cops already investigated the Doom Rider."

"Then we're looking for anything they missed," Frank said.

"Well, it wasn't the cars that malfunctioned," I said. "And it wasn't the tracks. It was one of the tunnels."

Frank glanced around. "I see one tunnel on the other side of the coaster," he said.

"And there's another one right over there." I pointed to a fake mountain made of some kind of plaster. The coaster tracks shot through it about fifteen yards from where we stood. "Let's check out that one first."

We made our way along the tracks until we reached the tunnel. It was at least ten feet off the ground, so we had to climb the tracks like a ladder to get inside. The tunnel wasn't very long—only about twenty feet or so. The fake mountain arched up and over the coaster, but the ceiling was low. I love when roller coasters plunge into a tunnel—the ride designers make it look as if you're going to crash right into something. My guess was that whoever designed the Doom Rider wanted this tunnel to give that impression too.

"Perfect," Frank said. "We picked the right tunnel on the first try." He inched along to a spot in the middle of the tunnel. "Here's where it collapsed."

I followed him to the place where the roof had fallen onto the tracks. There was plaster dust everywhere, so I pulled my T-shirt up over my mouth to help me breathe. A gigantic chunk of the hard plastic ceiling of the tunnel had fallen away from the metal bars that made up the frame. The blue sky peeked through, sun glinting off the tracks.

I let out a whistle. "This is serious damage."

"No wonder Maggie got killed when all this stuff fell on her," Frank said. "Her head would've been only a foot below the ceiling."

"There's no way she could've avoided being hit." I didn't like to think about that nice woman in such a scary situation.

"The police and the safety inspectors checked the roller coaster car, the safety restraints, and the tracks," Frank said.

"Yeah, but did they check the cave-in itself?" I asked. "From what it said on our mission disk, they only checked the coaster, not the cave-in. What would make something like this happen?" I stood up on the tracks and stuck my head through the hole in the roof. The edges of the plastic were sharp and twisted where the material had broken away, but none of the bars of the frame were broken. "It wasn't structural damage," I told Frank. "The steel bars are intact."

"So something made the hard plastic and the plaster decorations break," Frank said.

"And I think I know what caused it." From where I stood, I could see a small piece of thick red cardboard stuck on one of the sharp plastic shards. I stuck my arm carefully through the broken roof and snagged it. Then I jumped back down into the tunnel.

"What is it?" Frank asked.

"I think it's a piece of a spent shell," I told him. "From an M-80 firework."

"Could an M-80 have done this much damage?" Frank wondered.

I thought about it. "An illegal M-80 could. They can contain as much as two grams of flash powder. That's why they're illegal—they're dangerous."

"People still sell them, though," Frank said in

disgust. "But don't you have to light an M-80 to make it go off? How could someone do that while speeding along on a roller coaster?" He frowned.

"You can set up a slow-burning fuse," I replied. "Somebody could have planted the M-80 on the top of the scenery and lit a really long fuse. It just happened to burn out when Maggie's car was passing underneath."

Frank looked grim. "There's our answer. Maggie Soto's death was no accident. Somebody brought this roof right down on her head. On purpose."

I opened my mouth to answer him. But before I could say a word, a strong arm slipped around my neck. Someone was attacking from behind!

4.

AN EXPLOSIVE DISCOVERY

"What's going on here?" The man with his arm around Joe's neck didn't look happy. "Who are you kids?"

"My name is Frank Hardy," I said quickly. "And that's my brother, Joe." Our ATAC training had taught us that the best way to deal with a violent situation is to keep calm.

"What are you doing in here? Can't you read?"

"We saw the 'Keep Out' sign," I admitted. "Are you a security guard?"

"No!" the guy bellowed. "I own this place. And I want to know why you boys are sneaking around in my roller coaster when it's clearly closed." He squeezed Joe's neck harder. "Did you punks have

40

something to do with the accident last week? Did you come back to get rid of evidence?"

"No!" I cried.

"So you're Uncle Bernie," Joe choked out. "We were hoping we'd get to meet you."

Uncle Bernie seemed surprised to hear that—especially from someone he had in a choke hold. He relaxed his grip on Joe's throat but kept holding his arm. "How do you know who I am?" he asked.

"We came here to offer you our help," I said, thinking fast. "My brother and I are sort of amateur detectives. We've solved a lot of cases back in Bayport, where we live."

"What's that got to do with me?" Uncle Bernie growled.

"We read about the tragedy here last week," Joe said. "It was in all the papers."

"And we saw that the police ruled out foul play," I said. *Even though they were wrong,* I added silently.

"But they still didn't have an explanation for why the cave-in happened, did they?" Joe asked. "We thought we could help you figure it out."

Joe shot me a look, and I knew we were both thinking the same thing. After everything we'd heard today about Uncle Bernie, it didn't seem likely that he'd want our help. In fact, it was more likely that he'd been the one to explode the M-80 on his own ride. Maybe he wanted to get the park closed down so he could collect on the insurance money. Maybe he'd had a motive to kill Maggie Soto that the police didn't know about. I wasn't sure. But the one thing I knew for certain was that I didn't trust him.

"You two think you're smarter than the cops?" Uncle Bernie snorted.

"No," Joe said. "But we did find something that they missed." He held up the piece of red cardboard.

"What's that?" Uncle Bernie asked.

"We think it's part of an exploded M-80," I explained. "Probably an illegal one that had enough power to blow that hole in the ceiling."

Uncle Bernie glanced up at the twisted plastic and the sky above it. He sighed and let go of Joe's arm.

"I knew there was no safety violation," he mumbled. "But why would someone want to explode my roller coaster on purpose? I could get shut down for something like this."

He almost sounded sincere. Sincerely upset.

"This place means a lot to you, huh?" I asked.

"It's my whole life," Uncle Bernie answered. "I inherited the park from my dad, Bernard Jr. And he inherited it from *his* dad, the first Bernard. My grandfather founded the place. And we Bernies have been running it ever since."

"So you've never worked anywhere else?" Joe asked.

"Sure I did," Uncle Bernie said. "But when my father died, I came right back here to take over for him. It's what we do in this family. This amusement park is our legacy." His face puffed up with pride. "One day my son will inherit it, and he'll be the fourth Uncle Bernie in charge here."

"Your son's name is Bernard too?" I couldn't help thinking that would be confusing at a family reunion.

"Yep." Tears welled up in Uncle Bernie's eyes as he mentioned his kid. Hard to believe this gruff and nasty guy had it in him. "Little Bernie. He's twelve."

Uncle Bernie suddenly turned and punched the wall of the tunnel. More plaster came falling down around us. Joe coughed.

"Little Bernie was sitting right behind that lady," Uncle Bernie said. "Right there when this thing collapsed on her. I was afraid he'd be traumatized by what he saw."

I nodded sympathetically.

"But you say somebody exploded an M-80 on the roof?" Uncle Bernie shook his head. "That means someone wanted the collapse to happen. And maybe they weren't after that lady. Little Bernie was right there too. He could've been killed!"

"Maybe he was the real target all along," Joe said. He turned to me.

"I think we should talk to Little Bernie," I said.

44

Uncle Bernie nodded. "You boys go right ahead. He's probably hard at work somewhere in the park."

"Do you know where?" Joe asked.

"Not really. He rotates, does a little of everything." Uncle Bernie beamed as he talked about his son. "Tell him I said it's okay, otherwise he won't want to leave his post. He lives for this park—he'll be a terrific Uncle Bernie one day."

Uncle Bernie said good-bye and headed off for his office to make some phone calls.

"It's a little weird that he doesn't know where his own son is," I said. "Didn't he say the kid is only twelve?"

"He probably figures his son is safe in the amusement park," Joe replied. He squinted at something over my shoulder. "But I'm not so sure. Check that out."

I turned to see what Joe was looking at. The Ferris wheel was slowly jerking its way around in the start, stop, start, stop motion that meant it was still loading riders on.

"What?" I asked. "It's just a Ferris wheel." I hate those things. They're totally boring. But Joe loves Ferris wheels. "Something looks strange to me," Joe said. "See that woman?"

I put my hand up to shade my eyes from the

bright sunlight. Joe was pointing to a woman about halfway up one side of the Ferris wheel. She sat in a cart with her son, who looked to be about four or five years old. "What about her?" I asked.

"She's struggling." Joe studied the Ferris wheel for another second. Then he took off at a run.

"Whoa," I muttered. I sprinted after him. I knew that if my brother was running toward something, he was going to need backup.

"Look out!" Joe yelled, pushing his way through the line of people waiting for the ride.

"Hey! No cutting!" a guy about our age yelled.

Joe ignored him and shoved his way to the front. I followed.

"Shut down the ride," Joe told the girl at the foot of the wheel. She was about to close the door on a cart that had just been loaded with passengers.

"I-I don't control it," she said, surprised.

"Who does?" I asked.

"Tommy," she said. She gestured toward a guy sitting on a little metal chair about ten feet away. He was reading the newspaper, one hand resting on the lever that started and stopped the wheel.

I shot Joe a look. "I've got it," I said. I ran over to Tommy and pulled the newspaper down. "I need you to shut off the wheel," I told him. "Can you do that?"

He glanced up, confused. "Sure. But why?"

I didn't really know the answer to that. But one look over my shoulder showed me that Joe was pointing up at the woman and her son. "That lady is in some kind of trouble," I told Tommy.

He pulled a pair of binoculars from under his chair and trained them up at the wheel. Then he jumped to his feet. "The safety bar is open!" he cried.

I grabbed the binoculars and looked. Sure enough, the black bar that was supposed to be locked into place across the passengers' laps was hanging open in midair. The woman clung to her son, her eyes wide with terror as the little boy wailed. His mouth was open and tears ran down his cheeks. But from way down here, I couldn't even hear him.

"Call security," I ordered Tommy. "We've got to get them down."

"We can't move the wheel," he said. He pulled a metal locking device over the control lever. "They're already halfway up. In order to get their cart to the bottom, they'd have to go up over the top. There's more wind up there. And the motion of the wheel might swing the cart so much that they'd fall out."

"Can't you put the wheel in reverse?" I asked. That way, the woman and her son would be getting closer to the ground the entire time. If they fell, they might not be hurt as badly.

Tommy shook his head. "It doesn't go in reverse."

I jogged back over to Joe and the girl. "There's no way to lower them down," I told him.

"Then we'll have to go up there and get them," he said. "The little kid is so scared, he's squirming all over the place. I don't think she can hold him for much longer."

"But how will we get him down?" I asked. "We can't climb with the little boy in our arms."

"We need rope," Joe said.

I turned to Tommy. He was on his walkie-talkie, summoning security. But I didn't think we had time to wait for them to arrive.

"There's a hose in the emergency fire panel," the girl said. "Could you use that?"

I checked out the panel. It was a short metal cabinet bolted to the edge of the platform where we stood. Through the glass door, I could see a fire extinguisher and a flattened fire hose all wound up. Somewhere below the cabinet there must be a pipe to send water through the hose in case of a fire on the Ferris wheel.

"That will have to do," I said. "Let's just hope it's long enough."

Joe pulled his T-shirt down over his elbow and

smashed the glass front of the cabinet to get to the hose inside. As he unrolled it from its spool, I turned to the girl.

"Good idea," I told her.

She blushed and smiled up at me.

I turned away fast. I hate when girls look at me like that. It turns my brain to mush—and I needed my brain right now. I had a Ferris wheel to climb.

The hose reached its full length. It was still attached to the spool.

"We need it to be loose," Joe said.

I grabbed the hose, wrapped the end around the metal spool, and pulled it taut. Luckily the metal was sharp on the edges. With a sudden yank, I was able to snap the hose free.

"Let's go," Joe said. He slung the hose over his shoulder and ran to the edge of the platform.

"What's the plan?" I asked, following him.

"I think we both need to get up there," Joe called over his shoulder. He jumped up and grabbed one of the bars of the Ferris wheel, then pulled his legs up over it.

"One of us to hold the cart steady, the other to tie the rope around the boy?" I guessed.

"That's right." Joe climbed to the outside ring of the Ferris wheel. All the carts were attached to this ring by giant metal bolts. The ring itself was built

49

like a huge curved ladder, with steel slats running horizontally between the verticals. Joe began to climb it quickly.

I kept up with him. It was easy to climb at the beginning, just like playing on the monkey bars back in elementary school. But when the wheel started to curve, we had to hang from the slats, holding our weight with our arms and legs wrapped around the bars. It was much slower going that way.

"We need to get on the outside of the wheel," I told Joe. "So we can just crawl up the bars."

"Catch the hose," he replied. He let go of the bar with one hand and tossed the hose down to me. I managed to grab it as it fell through the air. I slipped it over my arm and took hold of the bar again.

Meanwhile Joe had pulled himself through two of the horizontal slats. He worked his way to the outside of the wheel, then reached down for the hose.

As soon as the weight of it was off my shoulder, I pulled myself up through the bars too. We hurried up the curve of the wheel on the outside.

The cart with the woman and her kid was almost at the top of the curve. As we got closer, I could see her frightened face. The little boy was still screaming and crying, squirming around in fear.

His mother held him with one arm and clung to the back of the cart with the other. I could see that she was getting tired.

"Please help," she called as soon as she spotted us. "I can't hold on for much longer!"

We put on a burst of speed and reached her cart. Joe tried to grab the safety bar to pull it back in, but it was swinging out from the cart. "It's too far away," he grunted.

"It won't close anyway," the woman said. "The lock is busted."

"Frank," Joe called. "I'll hold the cart steady. You get the rope around this boy."

I nodded, inching my way toward the cart as Joe tied one end of the hose around the rim of the metal Ferris wheel. He wrapped a loop or two around his own arm to help him stay balanced. Then he sat on the edge of the wheel and reached out for the cart. He grabbed the back of it with both hands and hung on.

I raced up to the cart. Standing on one of the metal slats, I leaned over the top of the cart and pulled the loose end of the hose toward me. I had to get the kid tied up fast. Joe wouldn't be able to hold us all still for long. I knew my brother and I could hold on if we needed to, and I figured the woman could, too.

But the little boy was so terrified that his eyes were squeezed shut and he thrashed around in fear. If he started to fall, he wouldn't be strong enough to grab onto something and hold himself up.

"It's okay, buddy," I told him. "We're gonna get you down." I slipped the free end of the rope around his waist and pulled it snugly around him. Then I wrapped it again so that another loop went between his legs. I tied it tightly around him so that the whole combination would work as a sort of seat for him to sit in.

The kid was so surprised to see me up there that he had stopped screaming for a second. His teary eyes met mine.

I grinned at him. "Don't worry," I said. "My brother and I are gonna lower you down the side now."

The kid's face paled. *Uh-oh,* I thought. *Is he going to start crying again?*

"We do this all the time," I told him, trying to make the whole thing sound like an adventure. "It'll be fun. It's just like mountain climbing."

The kid's chin trembled.

"Now you have to be brave while I lift you out over the side," I said. "You can be brave, can't you?"

The little boy blinked at me. Then he nodded.

"Okay. You be brave, don't worry, and you'll be down on the ground in no time." I reached in. He wrapped his arms around my neck and I lifted him out of his mother's embrace. She looked scared, but she reached out and grabbed onto the back of my shirt.

"In case you start to wobble," she explained. "I can try to hold you until you get your balance back."

I nodded. "Thanks." I hoped I wouldn't need the help. But it wasn't easy standing on the rim of the wheel like this. The wind whipped against my face.

"Is the rope tied tight?" I asked Joe.

"Yup," he said.

"Then here we go." I slowly turned toward the outside. I eased myself down into a sort of sitting position, with my back against the cart. Joe held the cart still, and the woman hung onto my shirt until I was braced against the wooden cart.

"Now you have to let go of me," I told the kid. "I'm going to swing you outside of the wheel."

He closed his eyes and let go.

I eased the hose down through my hands, slowly lowering the little boy down along the side of the Ferris wheel. I moved only an inch at a time—any more than that and he would've dropped too fast and gotten scared.

I looked up at Joe. He still had the hose looped around his arm.

I was out of rope. The little boy dangled ten feet above the ground. "I need some slack," I called to Joe.

He untangled his arm from the two loops of hose. I lowered the little boy down another foot.

His mother bit her lip. "What do we do now?"

I had no idea.

But down on the ground I spotted three security guards rushing around. "Help is here," I told the woman. "Security will know what to do."

I had a good view from up here. I saw one of the guards run over to a maintenance shed and pull out a ladder. He dragged it over to the Ferris wheel and they set it up under the little boy.

A guard climbed up and quickly untied the kid, handing him down to one of the others. Then he gave me a thumbs-up.

I relaxed my muscles. So did Joe. The kid was small, but it had still been a strain to hold him on the rope this whole time.

"Thank you," the woman breathed. "Thank you so much."

"We're going to climb back down," I told her.

"Will you be able to hold on if they move the Ferris wheel? The only way to get your cart to the bottom is to turn the ride on and send you up and over the top."

She nodded. "I'll be fine. It's just when I had to hold Devon that I couldn't hold on to the cart. Now it's no problem—I have both hands free."

"We'll see you at the bottom, then," Joe told her. He untied the hose, pulled it up, and slung it back over his shoulder.

We climbed back down the rim of the Ferris wheel.

At the bottom the little boy—Devon—ran up and gave me a high five.

Tommy turned the Ferris wheel on and moved it slowly around until Devon's mom reached the platform. The security guards helped her out, and Devon rushed into her arms.

Tommy went to check out the broken safety bar while one of the guards let the other riders off, and another guard put a RIDE CLOSED sign on the fence surrounding the Ferris wheel.

"That's two rides with mysterious problems," Joe murmured. "Do you think this was an incident of sabotage?"

"I don't know," I said. "I'm just glad we were here to help before anything too bad happened."

"We have to get to the bottom of this," Joe said.

"You're right. We need to get back to the investigation." I led the way toward the exit from the Ferris wheel. "Let's go talk to Uncle Bernie's son."

5.

THE REAL TARGET?

"Hey, can you help me?" I called to the cute girl at the concession cart. "I'm looking for Little Bernie Flaherty."

"Little Bernie?" Jonesy growled from his post at the end of the cart. He was busy pushing it past the fifty-foot-tall slide. "What do you want with him?"

"We just want to talk to him," Frank replied. "We're doing a paper on family businesses, and we hear he's going to inherit this place."

Jonesy laughed, but he didn't seem amused. "He'll inherit a broken-down dump. One more accident like that Ferris wheel thing—or the roller coaster last week—and they'll shut this death trap down."

"It's summer," the cute girl pointed out. "Why are you doing a paper?"

"Um . . . for extra credit," Frank said.

"Oh." She didn't seem so interested in talking to us now that Frank had made us seem like total nerds. What did I tell you? He's clueless around girls. "Little Bernie is in the ticket booth," she said.

Jonesy pushed the cart away from us, and I watched her disappear after him.

Frank headed over to the ticket booth. We'd already bought our admission tickets, but we waited on line anyway. No sense in getting everyone else in the line upset. When we got to the front, I had to stop and take another look.

No way was the guy in the ticket booth Little Bernie. Uncle Bernie had said his son was twelve years old. But this dude was gigantic! He had to weigh at least three hundred pounds and he was so tall that his head almost brushed the ceiling of the booth.

"She sent us to the wrong guy," I whispered to Frank as we approached.

"I don't think so," Frank murmured. He grinned at the ticket seller. "Are you Bernard Flaherty the Fourth?"

The guy grunted. "Who wants to know?"

"I'm Joe Hardy and this is my brother, Frank," I

58

said. "Uncle Bernie said we could talk to his son about the accident last week."

"Is that you?" Frank asked.

"Yeah. I'm Little Bernie."

I had to look down at my feet to keep from laughing. Little Bernie was the biggest person we'd seen all day!

"How old are you?" Frank asked.

"I'm almost thirteen," Little Bernie said. He rolled his eyes. "Don't tell me, I know—I'm big for my age."

"You sure are," I said. "When I was twelve I was totally puny."

"So my dad told you to hang out with me?" Little Bernie asked. "Cool!"

He grabbed the shade that was hung above him and pulled it down over the window. On the outside, the word CLOSED was written in fading paint. Little Bernie stepped out the side door of the ticket booth.

"Let's go," he said cheerfully.

I glanced back at the people waiting in line. "What about your customers?" I asked.

Little Bernie shrugged. "They'll wait."

"That doesn't seem fair," Frank said.

"Oh, all right," Little Bernie grumbled. "I'll send someone over to cover for me." He stuck his head back inside the booth and picked up a phone.

While he called for backup, I pulled Frank aside. "I can't believe he's only a kid," I said.

"Some people grow faster than others," Frank pointed out. "But it seems like he's inherited his lack of charm from his father."

"Yeah," I said. "I wonder what else runs in the family."

Little Bernie came back out and let the door slam closed behind him. "Someone will be here soon," he said. "You guys want some cotton candy?"

"Sure." I followed Little Bernie back into the amusement park. I felt bad for the line of people waiting to buy tickets, but what else could we do about it?

"Aren't you too young to be working here?" Frank asked.

"Yeah. That's why I don't get paid," Little Bernie said. "I don't really work at the park . . . officially."

"But you were selling tickets," I pointed out.

"Duh," he said. "My dad makes me work in different jobs all over the stupid park. He says I'll learn the ropes that way."

"You mean you'll learn the amusement park business?" Frank said. "So you'll know how to run the place someday?"

SUSPECT PROFILE

<u>Name</u>: Bernard Flaherty IV

<u>Hometown</u>: Holyoke, Massachusetts

<u>Physical description</u>: Age 12, 6', 304 lbs. Frizzy red hair, pale skin.

<u>Occupation</u>: Seventh grade student; works at Uncle Bernie's Fun Park.

<u>Background</u>: Child of divorce. Mom left.

<u>Suspicious behavior</u>: Doesn't care about his family's amusement park.

<u>Suspected of</u>: Sabotaging the Doom Rider roller coaster.

<u>Possible motives</u>: Resents his father.

"Yeah." Little Bernie stopped at another one of the wooden concession carts. This wasn't the one with Jonesy and the cute girl. A gruff older woman manned this cart.

"Three cotton candies," Little Bernie told her.

She handed them over with a sour look on her face.

Frank reached for his wallet.

"No way," Little Bernie told him. "You're with me. And mine are free because I practically own this dump." He sneered at the woman. "Now get back to work," he said in a fake stern voice. Then he laughed at his own "joke." The sour-faced woman turned away, annoyed.

Little Bernie might not *look* twelve years old, but he sure acted like it.

"Thanks for the cotton candy," Frank said. "It must be cool to get all this stuff for free."

"I guess." Little Bernie grabbed a handful of cotton candy and shoved it in his mouth. "I get to go on all the rides, too. As many times as I want."

"That's awesome," I said truthfully.

"I know," Little Bernie replied.

"So you spend lots of time here?" Frank asked. "Even during the school year?"

"Every day after school," Little Bernie said. "We have to close the park for three months in the winter because it gets too cold. But otherwise me and my dad are always here. It's like we live here."

I stuck some cotton candy in my mouth and waited until it melted away. I couldn't tell if Little Bernie was bragging or complaining about his life at the park.

"Where's your mom?" I asked.

"She left," he said. "She used to work here too, but she got sick of it. She wanted my dad to let someone else run it."

"And he wouldn't?" Frank asked.

"Are you kidding?" Little Bernie scoffed. "This place is the only thing my dad cares about. That's why they got divorced. She said he loved the park more than her."

"Do you live with your dad?" I thought I knew the answer to that one already. Uncle Bernie didn't seem like the kind of guy who'd let his son grow up away from the family amusement park.

"Yeah. I see my mom on weekends." Little Bernie downed the rest of his cotton candy. "Dad wants to make sure I know how to run the fun park. He didn't want Mom moving me to some other state or anything."

Now I *knew* he was complaining.

"That must be tough," I said.

Little Bernie blushed. "No way," he replied. "I have the perfect life. Most of the kids at school only get to go to an amusement park like once a year. If they're lucky! But I get to be here all the time!"

"I bet you know every nook and cranny of the park," Frank said admiringly.

"Definitely," Little Bernie bragged. "I know some stuff even my dad doesn't know."

"Like what?" I couldn't help but ask.

Little Bernie lowered his voice as if he were

telling us some big secret. "Well, most of the rides have, like, basements below them."

I thought about the "basement" we'd found underneath the Doom Rider. I nodded.

"The basements are connected by all these little tunnels!" Little Bernie added excitedly. "They used to be for maintenance, I guess, but no one has used them in years. You can get all over the park without ever going above ground."

Frank raised his eyebrows. I knew what he was thinking: Tunnels like that could be very useful if you were trying to sabotage the amusement park rides without getting caught. Still, I doubted that Uncle Bernie was really in the dark about those tunnels. Little Bernie might think his dad didn't know about them, but I had gotten the sense that Uncle Bernie knew the park like the back of his hand.

Little Bernie seemed to be waiting for an answer. "Wow," I said. "That's really cool. Can you show us?"

He shook his head. "Are you crazy? I would get in huge trouble if I took you guys backstage. Customers are only supposed to see the face of the park, that's what Dad says. They're never supposed to see how things really work or it spoils the illusion."

"Okay," I said. I didn't bother to tell him we'd

already been "backstage" today. "So listen . . . did you see anybody climbing on the roller coaster last week?"

Little Bernie blinked in surprise. He'd obviously forgotten that Frank and I were here to talk about the accident.

"Uh . . . no," he said. "Why would someone climb on it?"

"We think somebody set off a firecracker and it caused the roof to collapse," Frank explained.

Little Bernie looked doubtful. "Must've been a pretty big firecracker," he said.

"Yeah, it was. More like a weapon," I told him. "Lots of people think firecrackers are toys, but they can do serious damage. And this one was probably more powerful than what's legally allowed."

"Wow." Little Bernie's eyes were wide. "It *was* loud. I thought the noise was just from the ceiling falling down. But I guess it could've been an explosion."

"Your dad told us you were right behind the woman who got hit," Frank said.

Little Bernie nodded.

"I . . . I don't want to scare you," Frank began.

Little Bernie puffed his chest out. "Nothing scares me."

Frank shot me a questioning look. I nodded.

Little Bernie was just a kid, but if he was in danger, he had the right to know.

"Well, we were thinking maybe somebody was trying to harm you instead," Frank told him.

Little Bernie gulped. "M-me?"

"Can you think of anyone who might want to hurt you?" I asked.

"Sure," he said. "Lots of people."

"Like who?"

"Well, there's that Richardson guy."

Frank pulled out the little notebook he carries everywhere. "Who's Richardson?"

"He's this loser who wants to buy out my dad," Little Bernie said. "He keeps trying to get Dad to sell him the park."

That didn't sound like something Uncle Bernie would want to happen. But I didn't see what it had to do with Little Bernie. "Why would Richardson want to hurt *you*?" I asked.

Little Bernie shrugged. "I don't know. Maybe he's just trying to scare my dad into selling. Or he wants it to look like the rides are dangerous or something."

"If the park was forced to close, Uncle Bernie probably would be more willing to sell it," Frank said. "Who else might want to hurt you, Bernie?"

Little Bernie scratched his mass of red hair.

"Uh . . . this kid from school really hates me. I had to kick him out of the amusement park a couple of weeks ago."

"How come?" I asked.

"He was getting rowdy, causing all kinds of trouble." Little Bernie tried to look tough as he said that, but it didn't really work.

"What's his name?" Frank asked.

"Chris Oberlander. He's a punk, that's what my dad says. I caught him spray painting on the walls of the boys' room."

"What was he painting?" Frank asked.

Little Bernie blushed. "Uh . . . pictures of me. My head on a pig's body. But that's not all. He also threw a match into a trash can."

"Sounds like trouble," I agreed. "Anyone else?"

"Yeah, there's Big Jim. He runs the snack bar. He might try to get me."

"Why would he be after you?" I asked.

"'Cause he's a know-it-all. He's been working at the snack bar for thirty years, so he thinks he's a total expert on the fun park."

"He probably is," Frank said.

"So what?" Little Bernie replied. "I'm still the one who's gonna own it. So he doesn't like me. He tries to charge me for hot dogs and everything. Can you believe that?"

I shrugged. I could believe it.

"What about people who would like to see the park get closed down?" Frank asked. "Maybe whoever set off the explosion wasn't trying to hurt you at all. Maybe they just wanted to make Uncle Bernie's Fun Park seem unsafe. This Richardson guy is a suspect like that. Can you think of anyone else?"

Little Bernie frowned. "My mom, I guess," he said slowly. "Her name's Karen. She'd probably get half the money if the park got sold. But she wouldn't do anything like that. Especially not with me on the roller coaster."

"Probably not," I agreed. But I noticed that Frank wrote down her name anyway.

"Okay. Thanks for your help, Bernie," Frank said.

"Are you guys gonna take off now?" Little Bernie asked.

"Yeah, we have to check out all the people you just told us about," I told him. But before I could even take a step, an ear-piercing scream rang out.

6.

NOT-SO-MERRY-GO-ROUND

Another scream rang out, and the sounds of people shouting filled the air. Two men raced past us.

"They're heading for the carousel!" Joe cried. He took off running, and I followed. I heard Little Bernie huffing along behind us.

When we reached the carousel, I had to push my way through a crowd of people just to see what was happening. I couldn't believe it—the thing was spinning out of control! Where was the carousel operator?

"Is it supposed to go that fast?" I asked Little Bernie.

He shook his head. "No way. But it's been running fine since 1935. I don't know what's wrong with it to make it go so fast now."

"We have to stop it," Joe said. "People might get hurt."

On the carousel, I saw the worried faces of mothers whizzing by. The kids on their painted horses were crying. One little boy puked over the side of the ride.

"Bernie, do you know where the controls are?" I asked.

Little Bernie was watching the out-of-control ride, shocked. "Uh . . . yeah. But they're inside. I mean, they're in the middle of the carousel. There's no way to get to them while it's turning."

Just then, the carousel operator came running back, looking panicked. "What's going on?" he shouted, then turned to Bernie. "I had to go so bad I couldn't wait—just left for a second. How could this happen?"

I looked at Joe just as he rolled his eyes. What kind of guy would leave a ride full of kids running? This place had problems—big problems. A baseball cap came flying through the air. The carousel was going faster and faster. I saw a woman's pocketbook get pulled off her arm by the centrifugal force created by the wild ride. Popcorn flew through the air, yanked out of the tubs the kids on the merry-go-round were holding.

The carousel spun even faster. The tinkly music

started to sound warped as the ride whooshed by.

"Look out!" Joe yelled as a camcorder came flying toward me. I ducked just in time.

"Somebody stop that thing!" a nearby father shouted. His face was white with fear.

A loud scream caught my attention. I saw a girl—maybe ten years old—hanging on to one of the poles at the edge of the merry-go-round. One foot was off the ride, and the wind was pulling her harder every second. She couldn't hold on much longer.

On the next go-round, she was going to fall for sure.

I glanced around the area. People were everywhere, screaming, crying—all watching the carousel. Even the park workers had abandoned their booths and carts.

Finally I spotted what I was looking for. A game booth had a bunch of stuffed animal prizes hanging from the top of it.

I sprinted over to the booth, leaped up, and grabbed the largest animal I could find—an enormous stuffed bear.

The girl was still screaming.

A glance over my shoulder showed me that she was already falling off the ride.

"Joe!" I yelled. "Think fast!" I hurled the bear at him.

Joe jumped into the air, grabbed the bear, and threw it to the ground just as the girl went flying off the carousel. She winged through the air, screaming the whole way.

Then she landed on the bear.

I drew a huge sigh of relief. Joe shot me a thumbs-up.

The girl's mother ran over to pick her up. As they hugged, the girl was still crying. But she hadn't been hurt at all.

Still, we couldn't relax. The ride was still spinning way too fast, and before we knew it other people would fall off too.

"There's a horse coming loose!" someone yelled.

Sure enough, one of the poles holding the painted horses had been jarred loose from the top of the carousel. It was going to come off any second.

"Hit the dirt!" Joe bellowed.

Everyone around us dropped to the ground, covering their heads. I heard a sickening creaking sound, then the horse—still on its pole—sped through the air over my head.

The pole speared one of the wooden concession carts, knocking it onto its side.

"Cool!" Little Bernie cried.

"We're just lucky no one was on that horse," I told him.

This was getting serious.

"Let's go," I told Joe as I ran past him. I took a leap and landed on the carousel, lying on my side. The force of impact and the speed of the ride made me roll along the floor, banging into the poles of the horses. From here, the velocity of the thing seemed even greater. The faces of the people watching were just a blur as they whirled past.

I spotted Joe getting ready to jump. I stood up and pulled my way along by the poles. When he jumped on, I was there to grab him so he didn't get thrown right off again.

"We have to get to the middle," I shouted. But the wind whipped the words right out of my mouth.

"What?" Joe yelled. I couldn't hear him over the crazy music and the noise from the spinning ride. But I could read his lips.

I pointed to the center of the carousel. That's where Little Bernie had said the controls were.

Joe nodded.

We had to get there. But it wasn't easy. The centrifugal force from the ride was pulling everything—and everyone—toward the outside edge of the platform. But we were trying to get to the *inside* edge. All the force of the wind and the ride were working against us.

I grabbed onto the nearest pole. I wrapped my arm around it and hung on with all my might. Then I held out my other hand to Joe.

He grabbed my wrist and I grabbed his.

Using me to stabilize him, Joe let go of the cart he was hanging on to. Immediately, I felt him wobble backward. The ride was trying to force him to the edge. I held on tight to the pole and to my brother, straining the muscles in my arms.

Little by little, Joe made his way forward against the centrifugal force. When he reached the pole behind me, he grabbed on. I let my muscles relax for a second while Joe wrapped his arm around that pole. Then he reached out for me.

We did the whole thing again, this time with me pulling myself along using Joe to stabilize me. With his help I got to the pole on the very inside edge of the platform. I grabbed on, then pulled Joe along until he was beside me.

We eased our way down the pole until we were sitting on the floor. The force of the ride was even stronger here. I fought against it, reaching toward the edge of the platform. I grabbed it as hard as I could and held on while I lay down on my stomach. My legs stretched back along the floor. I held on to the inner edge of the platform for dear life.

Next to me Joe did the same thing.

From that position I could see the machinery of the carousel. Well, I could see where it was, anyway. We were spinning around so fast that the machine looked like a blur of black and gray. It was impossible to tell what was wrong with it.

Sparks shot off the mechanism as we spun even faster.

"It smells like something's burning," Joe yelled above the noise of the ride.

"We have to stop this thing before it blows," I yelled back.

I squinted at the machine. There was a wire—a thick orange wire like the one Dad uses as an extension cord when he puts up the Christmas lights outside the house. As we whirled around the center, I kept my eyes on that orange line. After about five spins around, I was sure: The wire led away from the carousel machinery.

"There's an extension cord," I shouted to Joe.

"I see it," he replied. "It leads underneath the ride. It must go out to the park somewhere."

"You think that's normal?"

"Who knows?" Joe yelled.

I sure didn't know anything about how amusement park rides worked. But it seemed strange that someone would need to plug in the carousel. My best guess was that the orange cord was somehow responsible for the ride going out of control.

"I'm gonna pull the plug," I yelled. "You have to keep me steady."

"Right!" Joe managed to undo his belt while holding on to the platform with one hand. As he pulled it out of the loops, the belt was torn from his grip by the force of the ride. It slithered toward the edge of the platform.

I slammed my sneaker down on it, pinning the belt to the ground. Never lifting my foot, I bent my leg and drew the belt toward me.

Finally Joe was able to grab the belt. He yanked it up to the pole and looped it around. Somehow he managed to get it buckled around the pole and his leg. He made it as tight as he could, then shot me a look. "In case I have to let go of the pole to hold on to you," he explained. "As long as I'm tied on, we won't fall."

"If you say so." I wasn't sure his plan would work. But the first thing we learned in our ATAC training was that you always need to take safety precautions.

Still holding on to the pole with one hand, Joe reached out and grabbed the back of my belt. He held me steady as I let go of the platform and leaned out toward the machine in the middle.

The centrifugal force was trying to yank me backward and sideways all at once. Joe held on, but I knew he couldn't do it for long. The force was too strong.

The orange cord whizzed by in front of me. I grabbed . . . and missed.

In no time we were back around. I grabbed for it again. My hand grazed the cord. I saw the orange line move a foot or so. Then the ride pulled me away from it again.

"Frank, come on!" Joe yelled.

I knew he couldn't hold on to me much longer.

The orange cord came by again. I stuck out both my hands and lunged toward it.

Success! The cord jumped off the ground and came spinning around with me. It felt hot in my hands.

But the ride kept spinning. The cord wrapped once around the machinery, then tightened.

"Uh-oh," I said.

"Let go!" Joe yelled.

I released the cord just as it snapped taut. The ride kept spinning, but the cord stayed where it was. If I'd still been holding on, it would have pulled me to a stop so fast I'd have gotten whiplash.

I tumbled backward past Joe. I was rolling toward the edge of the platform. I grabbed the first thing I saw—the hoof of a painted wooden horse—and held on.

Back in the machinery, the cord was still wrapped around as the machine spun. Sparks flew out from the friction between the cord and the metal.

Then the cord snapped.

There was a small explosion somewhere behind me, and the carousel began to slow down.

Slowly the music returned to normal.

Slowly the force pulling us toward the edge lessened.

Slowly the people watching stopped screaming.

But the ride didn't stop. It was back to normal merry-go-round speed, but it just kept going.

"Let us off of this thing," a mother holding a toddler begged.

Joe unbuckled his belt from the pole, hopped up from the platform, and jumped down into the middle of the ride. He grabbed a giant lever and pulled it.

"The ride is still on," he called to me. "I turned it off!"

I laughed. After all that, the carousel's simple on-and-off switch still worked.

The ride slowed to a halt, and the crowd rushed

forward to help people off. Joe climbed back up onto the platform and slapped me on the back.

"I know I always say carousels are boring," he told me. "But that was the best ride ever!"

7.

INNOCENT BYSTANDER

"You guys are so cool!" Little Bernie cried, rushing up to us. "What went wrong with the ride?"

"I'm still not sure," I admitted.

"I heard an explosion from somewhere behind me after the cord snapped," Frank said. "Somewhere away from the carousel itself."

"Let's go see," I said. I made my way through the crowd of hugging people and crying children. Then I circled the merry-go-round until I found what I was looking for—the orange cord. It came out from underneath the carousel just as I had suspected. I followed it across the walkway and to a locked utility closet. The cord ran under the door and disappeared inside. "Can you open this door?" I asked Little Bernie.

"No problem. I have a passkey," he boasted. He pulled a key from a chain around his neck and unlocked the closet. "No way," he breathed.

Inside, attached to the orange cord, was a power generator.

"Someone hooked a generator to the carousel to make it spin faster," Frank said. "But who—"

A siren ripped through the air.

We spun around to see an ambulance come screeching into the crowd of people. Two EMTs leaped out of the back and rushed over to a guy lying on his back near the harpooned concession cart.

"Oh, no," Frank said. "Did he get thrown from the carousel?"

By the time we got through the crowd of gawkers and reached the ambulance, the EMTs were already pulling a sheet over the man's body.

"What happened?" I asked.

"We're not sure," the EMT replied. "Looks like a heart attack."

"Was he on that carousel?" Frank asked.

I peered down at the poor man. Then I kneeled and took a closer look. "This wasn't caused by the carousel," I said. "He's got a bee crushed in his hand."

The EMT knelt next to me. "Where?"

I pointed it out. The EMT turned the guy's hand over, revealing a tiny swollen hole. "The bee stung him, he crushed it, and then he died," the EMT said. "Looks like the bee might be related to his death."

"He must've been allergic to bees," I guessed. "He went into anaphylactic shock, and nobody noticed in all the hysteria about the out-of-control carousel."

"Then his death was still caused by the sabotage to the carousel," Frank said grimly. "At least indirectly. If people hadn't been distracted by the ride, someone might have noticed that this man needed help."

"It's true. If we'd gotten here sooner, we could've given him a shot of adrenaline and saved his life," the EMT said.

"You don't know that," Little Bernie put in. "It's not fair to blame the carousel."

"It's yet another example of unsafe rides at this amusement park!" a loud voice broke into our conversation. "This is the second accident in two weeks!"

It was a tall man in a dark suit and tie. His face was bright red and sweaty. *That's what he gets for wearing a suit on a hot summer day,* I thought.

"You!" the man shouted, pointing at Little

Bernie. "You should be ashamed of your father, allowing this run-down old park to stay open."

"Who let you in?" Little Bernie demanded. "Security!"

"I paid for a ticket like anybody else," the man said. He raised his voice, trying to get the attention of the other people gathered around the carousel. "This place should be shut down! How many people have to die here before the state takes action? Somebody should sue them!"

"Who is this guy?" I asked Little Bernie.

"John Richardson," he told me. "Security!"

So this was the businessman Little Bernie had told us about earlier. The one who had a motive to hurt him.

"What's going on here?" Uncle Bernie came huffing and puffing over to where we stood.

"You've had another accident on one of the rides, Flaherty," John Richardson said loudly.

"No one was injured on the carousel," I told Uncle Bernie. "But—"

"Richardson, I thought I told you to stay away from this park," Uncle Bernie interrupted. He didn't seem to want to hear about the carousel disaster.

"If I were you, I would seriously reconsider the offer my company made you," Richardson said more quietly. "My offer of a million dollars is the best one you're going to get for this place."

"Yeah, so you can turn it into a strip mall or a condo park or some other ugly piece of suburban sprawl," Uncle Bernie spat.

"I want to turn it into a parking garage, actually," Mr. Richardson said.

Uncle Bernie looked ready to explode. "A *garage*? Are you crazy? This park has been in my family since 1924! It's my whole life, and my father's and his father's. It will be my son's one day. And you think I'm gonna let you turn it into a *garage*?"

"Look, Flaherty," Mr. Richardson said. His face was getting red again. "It's only a matter of time before you get shut down for all these safety violations—"

"There haven't been any violations," Uncle Bernie interrupted. He glanced nervously at the people standing nearby. Most of them were watching this conversation with interest. "These incidents were accidents, plain and simple."

"—and once the park is closed, our offer to buy it will be a lot less money," Mr. Richardson continued. "You'll be begging us to take it off your hands."

"Do you think we really can sue him?" a woman asked Mr. Richardson. "My daughter's hands got all scraped up from holding on to the merry-go-round when it was out of control."

"Yeah, and one of the carousel horses banged up my knee," a nearby kid added.

Uncle Bernie's eyes bulged. I could see that he was about to panic.

"Hey, Dad," Little Bernie said, tugging on his sleeve.

But Uncle Bernie ignored him. He shook off his son's hand and climbed up onto the carousel. "Attention, everyone!" he yelled.

"This ought to be good," Frank murmured. "How's he gonna make all these people forget about wanting to sue him?"

"I apologize for the unfortunate malfunction on our carousel," Uncle Bernie announced. "We here at Uncle Bernie's Fun Park take your safety very seriously. And that means the carousel will be closed until we can find out exactly what happened."

"You mean exactly who hooked it up to some extra juice," I said.

"In the meantime, to show how sorry we are, I'd like to offer everyone in the park a hot dog on the house."

The murmuring of the crowd grew more cheerful.

"In fact, I'll throw in a free ice cream cone for each kid, too," Uncle Bernie added.

Immediately a cheer went up from all the kids in the crowd. People streamed toward the snack bar, smiles on their faces.

"Wow," Frank said. "Looks like all it takes is a free hot dog and people will forgive anything."

"Not me," I replied. "I still want to get to the bottom of these so-called accidents. Although I wouldn't mind a free hot dog first."

I glanced over at Little Bernie. He was smirking at John Richardson, and Mr. Richardson didn't look too happy about it.

"Don't go gloating yet, kid," Richardson said. "This place will be mine, one way or another." He stalked off.

Little Bernie grinned at me. "That guy's such a loser," he said. "You dudes want a hot dog? I can take you to the front of the line."

"Sure," I replied. We followed him over to the snack bar. Normally I'd feel bad about cutting in line, but everybody there seemed happy to let us go first. Several of them slapped Frank and me on the back as we walked by. Even if they weren't planning to sue Uncle Bernie, they still considered us heroes for getting the carousel to stop.

The guy who served us our hot dogs didn't look too cheerful, though. He sneered at Little Bernie, and he sneered at us.

I didn't care. That dog hit the spot!

"What do you think about John Richardson?" Frank asked as we left the snack bar with our food. "He looks like a suspect to me."

SUSPECT PROFILE

Name: John Richardson

Hometown: Boston, Massachusetts

Physical description: Age 48, 5'10", 166 lbs. Thinning brown hair, face flushes easily.

Occupation: Land developer

Background: Unclear right now.

Suspicious behavior: Was present when carousel went out of control. Has made veiled threats to Uncle Bernie and Little Bernie.

Suspected of: Sabotaging the Doom Rider roller coaster and the carousel.

Possible motives: Wants Uncle Bernie to sell him the amusement park so he can tear it down.

"Yep," I agreed. "It's obvious that Uncle Bernie isn't willing to sell to him. But if he got the amusement park closed down, Uncle Bernie would probably change his mind."

"You think so?" Little Bernie asked.

"Sure," Frank said. "If the park is really closed for good, your dad would have no reason to keep the land. He'd have to sell it and start over somewhere else."

Little Bernie stopped walking.

"What's up?" I asked.

He took another step, then staggered backward a little. "I . . . I don't feel so good," he said.

"Are you sick?" I asked. "What's wrong?"

"It's the . . . the . . ." Little Bernie's eyes rolled back in his head. Then he collapsed on the ground.

8.

ROTTEN MEAT

Little Bernie lay crumpled on the blacktop, uncon-scious.

Immediately I knelt by his side. I was grateful for my emergency medical training. "Bernie, can you hear me?" I asked. I lightly grabbed his shoul-der and repeated the question.

"No answer," Joe said. "Check his airway."

"Help me roll him." Little Bernie was too heavy for me to move quickly. Joe bent and helped me push him over until he lay flat on his back.

I tilted Little Bernie's head back and gently lifted his chin. I eased his mouth open a little. There was still no response.

"Is he breathing?" Joe asked.

I bent over Little Bernie's face and put my cheek

next to his nose and mouth. I watched his chest for signs of breathing. In a second I felt air coming from his mouth. His chest rose and fell. "Yeah, he's breathing." I put two fingers to Little Bernie's neck and felt for a pulse. "His pulse is strong," I told Joe.

"Okay, let's get him into the recovery position," Joe said.

I pulled Little Bernie toward me while Joe pushed from behind to help move him. As he rolled, I lifted his arm over his head and Joe crossed one of Little Bernie's ankles over the other. Soon enough we had him lying on his side. His knee had bent because of the crossed ankles, so he lay propped up by his knee and arm.

Joe and I stood up. At this point in the emergency medical treatment, we were supposed to go get help. But somehow I didn't think Little Bernie needed an ambulance. He was breathing fine, his pulse was normal, and his skin looked the same as ever. He hadn't grown pale, or flushed, or turned green or blue like he would have if there was something really wrong.

"Doesn't seem like he choked," Joe said. "He can breathe."

I nodded. "And if he'd gotten a bite of bad meat, his color would have changed. Or his pulse would be racing . . . or *something*."

Little Bernie's eyelids fluttered, then opened. "What happened?" he asked.

"I don't know," I told him. "What do you remember?"

Little Bernie slowly sat up. "I was eating a hot dog."

"Yeah. Then what?" I asked.

"Something tasted funny . . . and that's all I remember." He frowned. "Do you think it was poisoned? You said someone might be trying to hurt me, right?"

I glanced around. Practically everyone in the park was eating a hot dog right now, and nobody else was keeling over. So it wasn't likely that the hot dogs were bad, or poisoned. On the other hand, the guy who'd given us the dogs had been scowling at Little Bernie.

"It's possible that your hot dog did this to you," I said.

Joe nodded. "You were in the roller coaster when that accident happened, and you're the only one who got sick from the hot dog. It seems like the perp could be trying to target you."

"Well, if the hot dog was tampered with, that means somebody in the snack bar knows about it," I said. "And you told us the guy who runs the snack bar doesn't like you."

Little Bernie nodded. "Big Jim. He hates me."

"Joe and I will go have a talk with him," I said.

"Okay." Little Bernie got to his feet. "I better get back to work before my father notices me slacking off."

"Don't you want to swing by the nurse's office?" Joe asked. "To make sure you're okay?"

"Uh . . . nah," Little Bernie said. "I feel fine now."

"All right." I didn't see Uncle Bernie anywhere, so he didn't seem likely to notice Little Bernie. But I was done hanging out with this kid, anyway. We needed to do some hard-core investigating. "Go to the nurse if you start feeling sick again. See you later."

Little Bernie took off with a wave, and Joe and I headed for the snack bar.

The crowd of people looking for free hot dogs had finally died down, and we found the scowling guy wiping the countertop.

"Are you Big Jim?" I asked.

His scowl grew deeper. "Nobody calls me that except old Bernie. My name is James Buchanan."

It didn't seem like a good time to mention that Little Bernie also called him Big Jim.

"Sorry, Mr. Buchanan," I said.

"Do I look big to you?" he interrupted. "Old

Bernie thinks it's funny to kick people when they're down."

I wasn't sure what to say. Big Jim was only about five foot four, pretty short for a guy. He seemed to have some kind of issue about his height, so I decided to ignore his comment.

"You don't seem to like Uncle Bernie very much," I said.

Big Jim glared at me. "Like him? I hate him!"

"How about his son?" Joe put in. "Do you hate him, too?"

"Why shouldn't I?" Big Jim snapped. "That little brat acts like I work for *him*. I don't care who his father is, he should show some respect to his elders!"

"Did you know Little Bernie got sick just now?" I asked. "He ate one of your hot dogs, and then he just collapsed."

Big Jim leaned across the counter, still scowling. "And?" he said.

"And he said he got a funny taste in his mouth just before he passed out," I said.

"I see." Big Jim leaned closer to me. He might be a short guy, but he was still pretty intimidating. "So you think I slipped the brat a bad hot dog. Who are you kids?"

"We're looking into the accidents here in the

park," Joe replied. "We're sort of amateur detectives."

"Then go harass someone else!" Big Jim roared. "You punks listen to me: I've been making hot dogs for thirty years! My dogs are all beef and there's nothing wrong with them. It's bad business to go around poisoning your customers—especially when one of them is the owner's son. I'm no fool. I can't stand the idea of working for that Little Bernie one day, but I didn't poison him. Now get out!"

I shot Joe a look.

"Let's go," he said.

We took off.

Outside, Uncle Bernie's Fun Park was anything but fun. Every ride had a long line snaked around it, the air was thick with humidity, it had to be at least ninety-five degrees, most of the kids were whiny, and the parents looked miserable.

"I think we need a break from this place," Joe said.

"We haven't made any progress on the case," I pointed out. "We have a bunch of suspects, but no evidence."

"I know. That's why we have to clear our minds," Joe said. "Spend an hour or two not thinking about Uncle Bernie. Then we'll have a better perspective on things."

SUSPECT PROFILE

<u>Name</u>: James "Big Jim" Buchanan

<u>Hometown</u>: Riggs, Massachusetts

<u>Physical description</u>: Age 61, 5'4", 150 lbs.
Wiry frame, long hair in a ponytail, constant scowl
on his face.

<u>Occupation</u>: Manages the snack bar at Uncle
Bernie's Fun Park.

<u>Background</u>: Has been making hot dogs for thirty
years.

<u>Suspicious behavior</u>: May have poisoned Little
Bernie's hot dog.

<u>Suspected of</u>: Sabotaging the Doom Rider roller
coaster and the carousel. Poisoning Little Bernie.

<u>Possible motives</u>: Hates Uncle Bernie. Resents the
fact that Little Bernie will inherit the amusement
park.

I rolled my eyes. Joe is so obvious sometimes.
"All right, what do you really want to do?" I asked.

"There's a water park half a mile away," he said
with a huge grin. "We passed it on the way up, and
it's scorching out. Doesn't a water slide sound
sweet right now?"

I had to admit, it did.

Still, with water parks came girls. Girls in bathing suits. Girls Joe would want to flirt with. "I don't know," I said. "Maybe we should stay here and keep looking around."

A little kid wandered past us, wobbly from the teacup ride. He turned toward me—and puked all over the ground.

"Okay," I said. "Water park it is."

9.

DOWN THE WORMHOLE

Splash World. I could hardly believe Frank had agreed to come here. Water parks are the coolest things on the planet!

"This place has a surfing pool!" I said, studying the map of the park.

Frank was busy looking around. "It's a lot newer than Uncle Bernie's."

"Yeah," I said. "This information map says the place opened only two years ago."

"It must get a lot more business than Uncle Bernie's does," Frank said thoughtfully. "I wonder if the owners of Splash World are planning to expand. They'd need Uncle Bernie's land to do that."

Unreal. I was trying to forget about our mission

for an hour or two, but Frank brought it right along with us. "You're not supposed to think about Uncle Bernie right now," I said. "Or about Richardson, or Big Jim, or anybody else. We're here to have fun."

"Okay." Frank squinted at the map. "Let's go on the Roundabout River."

"You're such a baby," I scoffed. "That's for little kids. All you do is sit in a stupid tube and float around the park."

Frank rolled his eyes. "What do you want to do?"

"There's a four-story-tall water slide," I said. "And two covered slides. Those are the coolest."

"Excuse me," said a voice next to me. "Do you mind if we look at the map with you?"

I looked down to see two gorgeous girls around our age. One of them had long curly dark hair and big brown doe eyes. The other one was taller, with strawberry blond hair and long legs. They both wore bikinis.

And they were both looking at Frank.

"Sure. You can squeeze in here with *us*," I said pointedly, but it was no use. It was happening again: That mysterious magnetic power Frank seems to have over girls was drawing these two right over to him. It's just *not* fair.

"Thanks," the dark-haired girl said. They both stepped in front of us, and we all looked at the map for a few seconds.

"I think we should go on the Roundabout River," the tall one said. "What do you think, Lisa?"

Lisa—the brunette one—nodded. "That sounds like a good way to start. We can see the whole park from the river and then pick our next ride." She gazed up at Frank. "Do you guys want to come with us?"

"Sure," I said quickly. "We were planning to start with the Roundabout River too."

"We were not," Frank put in. "You said it was boring and that it was for little kids."

Lisa and her friend shot me dirty looks. I shot Frank a dirty look. Was he really so clueless? Did he seriously not get that I was trying to find an excuse to hang out with two cute girls?

"You don't have to come on it, then," Lisa told me. "Renee and I will go with your friend."

"He's my brother, actually," I said, putting on my best flirtatious smile. "And I was just teasing him about the ride."

"You were not," Frank argued. "You wanted to go on the covered water slides."

The tall girl—Renee—raised her eyebrows. "Those things are terrifying. You couldn't pay me to go on one of those. Let's go to the river, Lisa."

They walked off toward the Roundabout River, and I glared at Frank.

"What?" he said.

See? He's completely clueless.

"Nothing. Let's go to the covered slides," I grumbled. If we couldn't hang out with the cute girls, we might as well have fun.

The line for the Wormhole was kind of long, but I figured it was worth the wait to go on the biggest, twistiest covered slide in the park. The Wormhole was a supersteep one-person water slide with a black metal roof covering the whole thing. I couldn't even see where the slide ended, but I figured it shot you out over a deep pool somewhere else in the park. Most covered slides spit you out about ten feet above the water. So after a terrifying ride down a pitch-black slide, you get to have a little free fall to thrill you at the end.

"I love water parks," I said.

"I know," Frank replied. "You love them so much you don't even care that we've been on line for a half hour already."

"We're almost there," I said. "We're on the stairs now." Everybody knows once you're on the stairs up to the high platform of the slide, you're in the home stretch.

Even so, we waited for another fifteen minutes.

"You're gonna thank me for this," I promised Frank. "The information map said that the Wormhole slide changes direction three times while you're in the tube."

"So?"

"*So,* it's amazing," I said. "You're completely enclosed in the metal slide, you've got water running down your back, you can't see where you're going . . . you're totally at the mercy of the Wormhole."

"As long as it's wet, I'll be happy," Frank said. "It's way too hot out."

Finally we got to the top. From here I could see out over almost the whole park, with its wave pool and whitewater rafting creeks and the Roundabout River encircling all the other rides. The Wormhole was just a big black tube, a circular opening maybe three feet wide with only blackness inside.

I watched the kids in front of me as they disappeared into the tube one by one. The park worker at the ride instructed them to grab onto the top of the tube, stick their feet into it, and let go. As soon as they did, the force of the water rushing down the tube pulled them inside. They vanished into the blackness almost immediately.

The park worker waited for a minute or so and

then let the next person on. I knew you couldn't have two people in the tube at once, so the whole ride probably only lasted for a minute. But so what? It would be worth it.

I was next in line. I was so pumped. "Can I go in headfirst?" I asked the worker.

He just laughed. "No. Trust me, it'll be scary enough feet first."

"I hope so." I glanced at Frank. "See you on the other side!" Then I grabbed onto the top of the tube, stuck my feet into the Wormhole, and let go.

The water was freezing! It pulled me along so fast that before I knew it, the light from the entrance was gone and I was in total darkness, whipping along superfast. I could barely even tell where the top of the tube was—I didn't have time to think about anything.

Suddenly my feet hit a wall and my whole body jerked to the right.

I gasped in surprise. But before I could even catch my breath, my feet hit another wall. I jerked left.

And kept speeding downhill. There was one more turn to go . . . but when would it happen?

Just when I thought I couldn't fall any farther, my feet hit the wall again. I slid right around the turn.

My feet hit another wall. And stopped.

The sudden stop brought the weight of my whole body down onto my ankles. My knees buckled, and I started to fall. But the tube was so narrow that my knees hit one wall and my back hit the other. I stayed there, crouched, for a couple of seconds, just trying to catch my breath.

What was going on?

Keep calm, I told myself. That was the first rule of dealing with a crisis—every member of ATAC had it drummed into their heads. *Take stock of your surroundings, then figure it out from there.*

I was standing on a blockage in the tube. There were only supposed to be three turns, and I'd gone through all three. So this must be the bottom of the tube. But it was blocked.

I pushed down with my toes, then slid my feet around, trying to figure out what was blocking the tube. It was something smooth and flat that felt a little bit like the rubber they use to make trampolines.

Okay, that's not helpful, I thought. I tried to figure out some other details.

I wasn't standing straight up, as far as I could tell in the dark. The whole tunnel seemed to be at an angle so that I leaned more to the left than the right.

The tunnel was narrow—only one arm span across.

It was pitch black.

And water was pouring down on my head.

Uh-oh, I thought. Water ran down the length of the whole tunnel. And if the bottom was blocked, that meant the water couldn't escape. It would start to build up into a pool at the bottom.

I lifted one foot. Sure enough, the water had formed a puddle on top of the blockage. It was up above my ankle already, and rising fast.

I had to get rid of the blockage—fast—before the water backed up even further.

I stomped down as hard as I could. It didn't move. I braced my arms against the wall of the tunnel and stomped down with both feet at once. It still didn't budge. I tried a few more times. Nothing.

A sound came from the tunnel above me. Sort of a whooping yell.

My blood ran cold.

Frank!

The worker at the top had waited for a minute, then let Frank into the tube. Any second now, he was going to land on top of me!

It's okay, I thought. *Maybe the impact will knock this blockage loose.*

I flattened myself against the side of the tunnel and braced for the hit.

Frank's feet walloped me in the shoulder, and he crumpled on top of me, pushing me back down to my knees. The water sloshed up into my mouth.

"Hey!" Frank yelled.

I pushed at him. "Get off of me!"

He pushed against the side of the tunnel and scooted up enough for me to stand again. "What's going on?" he called down.

"The bottom of the tube is blocked," I said. "I can't push it loose. Even the weight of two of us didn't knock it free."

"That's bad," Frank said. "There's water coming down."

"I know."

"The water will fill the tube and we'll drown," Frank said.

"I know," I repeated. "We have to find a way out. Fast, before someone else comes down."

"They put up a chain behind me so the workers could change shifts," Frank said. "No one else will be down for at least a few minutes."

"Good. Then no one else is in danger," I said. "But we're still in deep trouble."

"If we can't go down, then we have to go back up," Frank called.

"How can we climb all the way back up?" I asked. "This thing is really steep. And what about all those turns?"

"I can reach the first turn from here," Frank said. "I'm gonna pull myself up over it."

The darkness was so total that I couldn't see him at all. But I felt the weight that had been pressing down on me ease as he pulled himself up.

The water had reached my waist now. I had to start climbing. But how? Every time I tried to push off the wall, my foot slipped against the smooth metal. The water made everything slick.

"I need a little help!" I called.

My brother's hand smacked me in the face.

"Sorry!" he said. "Grab on."

I grabbed onto his wrist. I figured he must be lying on his stomach above the turn. He pulled me up out of the water. I felt the tube change directions. Up here we could crawl forward, but the water rushing down made it difficult. In front of me, Frank lost his balance and was swept back down the tube.

"Look out!" he yelled.

I swiveled around and pushed my feet against the wall opposite me. This way I could block his path and keep him from falling back down to the bottom of the tube.

Oof! He slammed into me.

"I think I get to go first from now on," I complained. "That's twice I've had to break your fall."

"Joe, the water's up over the turn already," Frank said. "It's rising fast."

"Let's get going." I led the way, crawling along the tube until I reached the next turn. "These two turns were really close together," I called back to Frank. "Maybe we can put our feet on the first turn and then pull ourselves up on the next one."

"Yeah," Frank's voice reached me through the darkness. "But then the tube goes straight up for at least thirty feet. How are we gonna climb that?"

I pulled myself up onto the next turn. Extending my arms over my head, I felt the final turn of the tunnel. I dragged myself up until I could look straight up the rest of the tunnel. Up above—*way* up above—I spotted a tiny circle of light. "I can see the top!" I yelled.

"How can we get there?" Frank yelled back.

I took a deep breath and tried to assess the situation calmly, the way Dad always did. We had a narrow space, and an almost vertical climb. What should we do?

It hit me like a bolt of lightning.

"It's a chimney!" I called.

"What?"

"Like in rock climbing, when there's a crack in the rockface big enough to climb in. We can use our hands and feet to brace ourselves against the wall and inch our way up."

"Got it!" Frank called. "But we have to go fast. The water is rising."

I pulled myself the rest of the way up into the tunnel and stuck my foot against the wall, about knee-high. I leaned across and pushed both hands against the same wall. Then I bent my knee and lifted my other foot. I pressed that foot against the wall under my butt. I was suspended in the tunnel, holding myself up between my arms and legs. Pushing hard against both walls, I straightened my back leg and lifted my body as far as I could. Now that my bottom leg was straight, I bent the other one and stuck it against the wall in front of me at knee-height. I took a split second to rest, then did the whole thing again.

Slowly I inched up the tube. I heard Frank doing the same thing below me.

My arms and legs were aching with the effort, and my lungs were working overtime. But I kept my eyes on the little circle of light above. I tried to ignore the water pouring down on top of me. It made the tunnel slippery, so I had to push hard against the walls to avoid sliding down.

Finally I reached the top. The sunlight dazzled my eyes for a few seconds, so I stayed put in the tunnel to let my sight adjust.

"Hurry up, Joe!" Frank called from below. "The water's up to my legs."

With a final exertion, I pushed my back hard against the wall and moved one of my arms up to grab the top of the tunnel. I held on tight and pulled myself up and over the top. Then I collapsed on the platform and tried to catch my breath.

"Dude!" cried the park worker standing two feet away. I heard gasps from the people at the front of the line.

"My brother's in there," I said.

The worker rushed over to the tube and pulled Frank out. He dropped down next to me on the metal platform. "My biceps are aching," he muttered.

"Where did you dudes come from?" the worker demanded. "You're not supposed to climb back up the slide."

"The bottom is blocked," Frank said. "Don't let anyone else go in. We almost drowned."

The worker stared at us in shock for a moment, then looked back into the tunnel. When he saw the water almost to the top, he yanked the walkie-talkie from his belt and got help.

The people standing in line were evacuated from the platform and the stairway, and someone at the bottom of the slide removed the blockage. By that time Frank and I had recovered enough to talk to the Splash World security guard who'd come to take our statement.

"What was over the bottom of the slide?" I asked.

The guard was a middle-aged woman with a long blond braid down her back. She looked embarrassed. "Someone put the cover on," she admitted. "When the ride is closed, we put rubber covers on the top and bottom of the tunnel. To keep the raccoons out and make sure the slide doesn't get all mucked up with falling leaves and stuff."

"You mean somebody purposely closed off the end of the slide while people were going down it?" Frank asked. "We could've been killed. You're just lucky it was us and not some ten-year-old kids."

"I know." The guard frowned. "The story I'm getting is that the worker at the bottom thought the Wormhole was already closed for the shift change. He didn't think anyone else was coming down, so he put the cover on."

"Do they usually cover the slide during a shift change?" I asked.

"No," she replied. "But it was this guy's first day on the job. He says he got confused. Needless to say, he's been fired."

Frank and I exchanged a look. Had this worker really just made a mistake? Or was he trying to hurt us on purpose?

"Is the worker still here?" Frank asked.

The guard shook her head. "We had him escorted off the premises. Splash World takes safety violations very seriously—"

"Thanks, but we've heard this speech today already," I interrupted her. "Can you tell us the guy's name?"

"Marc Krakowski," she said.

Frank wrote the name in his notebook, and we made our way down the long staircase.

"It's too bad we can't talk to the worker who did this," Frank said. "I'd like to know if he's connected to Uncle Bernie's Fun Park in any way."

"We'll have to go back to Uncle Bernie's to find out," I said. "But first I could use a nice, boring ride on the Roundabout River."

We snagged some inner tubes and plopped ourselves in the slowly moving water. "Now this is the way to relax after some chimney-climbing," I joked. "What a workout!"

"We've got a problem," Frank said. "We have no

idea who's been sabotaging the rides at Uncle Bernie's—and maybe here, too. There's no way we'll be able to solve this thing and get back home today."

"Let's call Dad and tell him we're gonna crash up here," I suggested. "We passed at least five motels on the way to Uncle Bernie's."

After we got off the ride and changed back into regular clothes, we headed back out to our bikes.

It was quieter in the parking lot. I pulled out my cell phone and dialed home.

Luckily, Dad answered the phone. If it had been Mom or Aunt Trudy, I would have had to lie. And I hated lying to them.

"Hey, Dad," I said.

"Joe. Are you boys all right?" Dad sounded worried.

"We're fine." I glanced at Frank and he shook his head. I knew what he meant: Don't tell Dad about our near-death experience in the Wormhole. The last thing we wanted was to freak out our father. Besides, we *were* fine. We'd gotten out of the scrape like we always do.

"No problems," I said into the phone.

"Where are you?" Dad asked.

"Still up in Massachusetts," I said. "We're at an amusement park."

"I see." Dad doesn't say much, but then he doesn't have to. I could tell by his tone of voice that he knew we weren't here for fun. He never asks for details about our ATAC missions. But he always knows when we're on ATAC business.

"The thing is, we kind of lost track of time," I said. "We won't be able to make it all the way home tonight."

"Hmph," Dad said. "You're sure everything's okay?"

"Yeah," I said. "We just need a little more time. We thought we'd stay in a motel up here."

"All right," Dad replied. "I'll tell your mother she can expect you home tomorrow."

"Thanks, Dad," I said.

"Be careful, Joe," he told me. "Call if you need anything."

"We will. Bye."

I hung up and turned to Frank. "Well?" Frank asked.

"He's not happy," I sighed. "But he knows how it is on ATAC business. We'll get some sleep tonight. And then tomorrow we'll finish the mission and be home by dinnertime."

10.

WORKING OUT

"Are you gonna eat those pancakes?" Joe asked me the next morning at breakfast.

I was busy staring out the window of the diner, thinking about the situation at Uncle Bernie's Fun Park. Joe reached across the table, ready to grab my last two pancakes with his fork.

I pulled my plate away.

"There are two suspects left who we haven't actually met and questioned yet," I said.

"You're doing work over breakfast?" Joe groaned. "Okay, so we have Big Jim, and John Richardson, and both Bernies. Who else? What about that big guy, Jonesy? He really hates Uncle Bernie."

"Maybe," I said. "But I was talking about Uncle

Bernie's ex-wife, Karen," I said. "Remember, Little Bernie said she'd get half the money if the park was sold."

Joe shook his head. "I don't think so. She wouldn't put her own son in danger. Little Bernie almost got hit by the Doom Rider cave-in, and somebody may have tried to poison him yesterday. It's hard to believe his mom could be involved in any of that."

I agreed with him. Even Little Bernie had said his mother wouldn't do anything like sabotage the rides. "Okay, so we cross her off the suspect list for now. That leaves one person. The kid from Little Bernie's school."

"The one who got rowdy at the park until Little Bernie threw him out," Joe said. "What was his name?"

I checked my notebook. "Chris Oberlander."

Joe glanced around the diner. "Pay phone," he said, pointing. "I bet there's a local phone book."

We headed over to the phone and grabbed the book from the counter underneath. Joe flipped through to the O section. "There are two Oberlanders in Holyoke," he reported.

"Give me the first number," I said, picking up the phone.

I got an answering machine.

But when I called the second number, a woman picked up. Maybe it was Chris Oberlander's mother.

"Hi," I said, trying to sound younger. "Is Chris there?"

"No, he's not," she said. "He went to the gym. Is this Ryan?"

"Um, no. This is his friend Frank," I told her. "Chris goes to Gold's Gym, right?"

"Planet Fitness," she corrected me. "Should I tell Chris you called, Frank?"

"No, that's okay. I'll probably see him at the gym. Thanks!"

I hung up and gave Joe a thumbs-up. "Planet Fitness, here we come." We paid at the counter and hurried out to our bikes. It took twenty minutes to find Planet Fitness. We could have used the hyper-sensitive GPS on our bikes to find the gym, but it's much more fun to ride around on the motorcycles and just look for places. When I'm on my bike, I never want to get off it.

But soon enough we spotted the gym. It was a medium-sized building with floor-to-ceiling windows in the front. Inside I saw the usual assortment of exercise machines, free weights, and cardio equipment.

"I wonder if Chris Oberlander is a musclehead,"

Joe said. "That could be bad if he really has it in for Little Bernie."

On the front door was a flyer advertising free introductory sessions at the gym. I pointed it out to Joe on the way in.

"Hi! Welcome to Planet Fitness!" the girl at the front desk chirped. "How can I help you guys?"

"We're interested in the free introductory session," I told her. "We're thinking of joining."

"Great!" she said. "Just fill out these forms and you can use the facilities for the next hour."

"Thanks." I took the forms and we filled in our names and put fake addresses in Holyoke. The whole time I kept looking around the gym. Which of these bodybuilders was Chris Oberlander? None of them looked young enough to be in school with Little Bernie.

"Maybe Chris is a high schooler who knows Little Bernie," I suggested to Joe.

"Could be. At least there are two of us if we have to fight a bodybuilder," he joked.

We handed our forms to the girl at the desk. "Hey, can you tell us if Chris Oberlander is around?" Joe asked her.

"Sure," she said. "He's over there in Free Weights."

I looked where she was pointing. There were three huge guys lifting weights on the blue mats in the corner. "Which one?" I asked. "We're new in town and Chris is a friend of our father's. We're supposed to meet him here."

The girl smiled. "He's the one in the green shirt."

"Thanks." We headed over toward the big guys and the free weights. None of them wore a green shirt.

But the skinny little geek hidden behind them did.

Joe stopped short. "That little kid?" he asked.

I checked the guy out. He didn't look like he could lift a telephone off a receiver, much less a barbell. He was struggling to do a bicep curl with what had to be a two-pound weight.

"He's no killer," Joe said. "Let's just go question him."

"No, we should watch him first," I replied. "Just because he's a twerp doesn't make him harmless. None of the things that happened at Uncle Bernie's Fun Park required strength to pull off."

"True. So let's work out." Joe headed over to one of the treadmills, and I got on a stationary bike. From there we could keep an eye on Chris without him noticing us.

The kid was scrawny, but he was determined. His puny biceps bulged as he lifted his little weight over and over again. His eyes never left the image of his arms in the mirror. His face wore an expression of grim determination.

I was impressed. He was a skinny little kid, but he was trying really hard.

He worked out for another fifteen minutes, sweat pouring down his face. Then, exhausted, he dropped the dumbbell back down onto the rack and went to get a drink from the water fountain.

"I think he's done," I told Joe. "Let's go."

As we slowed down and got off our machines, Chris pulled a gym bag out of one of the lockers near the door. He took off his sweaty T-shirt, pulled a dry one out of the bag, put it on, and stuffed his wet shirt into a pocket on the bag. He then left the building. Joe and I followed.

Outside, Chris headed toward the bike rack. "Excuse me, Chris?" I called.

He jumped, glanced over his shoulder . . . and took off!

Joe shot me a surprised look, then ran after him. We followed him around the corner and halfway down the side street. He wasn't hard to catch—his legs were pretty short, after all.

But just as I reached out to grab him, Chris ducked under my hand and cut right. He sprinted into someone's yard.

I ran after him.

He jumped over a chain-link fence and circled back around toward the gym. "He's going for his bike," I called to my brother.

Joe nodded and ran back toward the gym while I followed Chris through an alleyway and up to Planet Fitness from behind. When he got back to the parking lot, Joe was there waiting for him.

Chris turned—and stopped short when he saw me behind him. He was cornered.

"Don't hurt me!" he wailed.

"I'm not going to hurt you," I told him. "We just want to ask you some questions."

"Do you always run when somebody calls your name?" Joe asked.

"You would too if people were always beating you up," Chris snapped. "Who are you guys?"

"My name is Frank and this is my brother, Joe," I said. "We were hoping we could talk to you about Little Bernie Flaherty."

"Little Bernie sent you?" Chris dropped his gym bag with a thud. He stuck his hands up in front of him, curled into fists. "What, now he's getting other people to come after me? He can't do it himself?"

"Chill," Joe said. "We're not gonna fight you. Put your hands down."

Chris kept his fists up and glared at us. "If you're

friends with Little Bernie, that means you're jerks. Because nobody decent would hang out with that idiot."

"We don't hang out with him," I explained. "We're just trying to figure out who might want to hurt him."

"That's easy," Chris said. "*I* want to hurt him!"

"You do?" Joe asked skeptically. "Why?"

"Because he's been picking on me since kindergarten," Chris said. "He's a big bully. I'm sick of it. Why do you think I'm working out?"

He bent down and unzipped his gym bag.

"Look," he said. He pulled out a huge bottle of vitamin supplements that read BUILD MUSCLE in huge type across the front. "I'm taking these, and I have this creatine powder that's supposed to help me bulk up. . . ." He pawed through a jumble of protein powders and other bodybuilding supplements. "One of these days I'm gonna be big enough to get back at Bernie."

I thought about Little Bernie. He was the biggest twelve-year-old I'd ever seen. Somehow I didn't think Chris Oberlander would ever be that big.

"How else are you trying to get back at him?" I asked.

Chris stopped looking through his bag. "Huh?" he said.

Name: Christopher Oberlander

Hometown: Holyoke, Massachusetts

Physical description: Age 12, 5', 98 lbs. Skinny, wears thick glasses with black frames.

Occupation: Middle school student

Background: Grew up tormenting by little Bernie.

Suspicious behavior: Heard to say that he wanted to hurt Little Bernie.

Suspected of: Sabotaging the Doom Rider roller coaster and the carousel. Poisoning Little Bernie.

Possible motives: Hates Little Bernie. Wants revenge for Little Bernie throwing him out of Uncle Bernie's Fun Park.

"We heard Little Bernie threw you out of the amusement park for making a scene a little while back," Joe said. "Have you tried to get revenge for that?"

"*He's* the one who made a scene," Chris grumbled. "I didn't do anything."

"But you're still mad at him, right?" I said. "Mad enough to try to kill him?"

Chris stared at me, confused. "Huh?" he said again.

"Someone has been tampering with the rides at Uncle Bernie's. Yesterday Little Bernie got a hot dog that may have been poisoned." I watched Chris's face for any sign of guilt. But he just looked surprised.

"He was poisoned? Did he die?" Chris asked hopefully.

"No!" Joe snapped. "Were you trying to kill him?"

"No way," Chris said. "I didn't know anything about it. I'm not even allowed back into the park—how could I have done any of that stuff?" He zipped his gym bag and stood up. "But if someone is trying to kill him, I hope it works."

Joe looked at me and shrugged. We obviously weren't going to get anything more out of this kid. I had a feeling that he was telling the truth, but you never know.

"Listen, stop taking those bodybuilding supplements," I told Chris. "You're never going to beat Little Bernie physically. The only way to deal with a bully is to stand up to him. Once you show him you're not afraid, he'll leave you alone."

"Easy for you to say," Chris muttered.

"Seriously, those supplements are bad for you,"

Joe said. "They don't really help, and some of them have dangerous side effects. You'll be much better off if you just eat right and keep working out. One of these days you'll have a growth spurt."

I grinned. He sounded just like Mom!

"And take some karate classes," Joe added. "If you know martial arts, it doesn't matter how big you are."

Okay, *that* didn't sound like Mom.

Chris headed off to the bicycle rack, and we went over to our motorcycles. Someone had stuffed a flyer into the seat of mine. I pulled it out.

"What next? Should we go find Little Bernie's mother?" Joe asked, straddling his bike.

"No," I said slowly. "We should go to the amusement park."

"How come?" Joe asked.

I showed him the piece of paper. It was no flyer. It was a note.

And it read, THE EVIDENCE YOU'RE LOOKING FOR IS IN THE HAUNTED HOUSE—A FRIEND.

11.

HALL OF HORROR

"It could be a trap," I said into the microphone in my bike helmet. Frank and I can talk to each other through our wireless mikes when we ride, and the noise-canceling helmets make it as simple and quiet as having a normal conversation. Well, a normal conversation while flying down the road with the wind in our faces and 130 horsepower between our legs. "Sometimes when you get a note from 'A Friend,' it's really from an enemy."

"I know," Frank's voice came through the speaker in my helmet. "But we have no choice. All we know so far is that everybody hates Uncle Bernie and Little Bernie, and lots of people would like to close the park down. But there's no smoking gun to lead us to one suspect."

"Then we'd better hope our smoking gun is in the haunted house," I said. "I love haunted houses, anyway."

I turned my bike into the parking lot of Uncle Bernie's Fun Park.

It was still pretty early—not even noon. The park wasn't crowded yet. The only line I saw was the line at the carousel. It was mostly teenagers. I guess everyone wanted to try out the wild merry-go-round after yesterday. I just hoped there wouldn't be a repeat of that unpleasant incident.

We made our way to the haunted house. The neon HALL OF HORROR sign was on, but there was no line. There wasn't even a park worker in sight.

"Do you think it's open?" Frank asked.

"It looks pretty deserted," I said. "But maybe our 'friend' wants it that way."

"Okay, let's go in." Frank led the way.

It was dark inside, like all haunted houses. But somehow after our adventure in the pitch-black Wormhole the day before, this darkness didn't seem so scary.

Spooky organ music drifted in through hidden speakers, and every so often a scream pierced the air. Usually in a haunted house, you hear other people screaming. But these were the canned screams that were part of the prerecorded soundtrack. As far as

I could tell, we were alone in the Hall of Horror.

Something grabbed my arm.

I jumped and spun around.

There was nothing there.

"Cool," I said, relaxing a little. Have I mentioned that I love haunted houses?

"Check it out," Frank said. In the dim light, I could see him pointing to the right. I looked over there and saw a dinner table all set up with fancy china dishes. In the middle was a man lying on a platter. His mouth was open, and an apple was stuck in it like he was the pig at a pig roast.

I chuckled. "That's gross," I said appreciatively.

"We're here to look for evidence, not to enjoy the haunted house," Frank reminded me.

"Oh. Right." I studied the fake dinner set for any sign of the evidence our "friend" had mentioned. But the table and chairs looked just like normal props. The man was obviously made of plastic.

Maybe the apple in his mouth was a reference to Little Bernie's poisoned hot dog? I shook my head. I was really grasping here to find whatever hint our "friend" had left for us.

I left the pathway and stepped over onto the dinner set to check it out.

"We're not supposed to go over there," Frank pointed out.

"No one else is here," I said. "And we're investigating, remember?"

"Just hurry up," he replied.

I got up close to the table and peered down at the apple. It was made of wax, like the fake fruits our Great Aunt May keeps in a bowl on her living room coffee table.

"Nothing here," I said, returning to the pathway.

We kept going.

I passed a portrait of a pretty girl hanging on the wall. It was lit by a small spotlight coming from the bottom.

I checked it out, because the girl was pretty.

But when I got up next to it, her face turned into the wrinkled face of an old hag. Then the flesh dropped off the face and it became a skeleton.

"Cool," I said.

I stopped to look at the picture more closely.

It changed back to the young girl, waited for about ten seconds, and then went through the girl-hag-skeleton process again.

I turned away. The effect was fun one time. But when you saw the whole thing happen again, it kind of lost its interest.

In front of me, a figure lunged from the darkness and grabbed Frank.

He let out a yell.

I ran to catch up, but by the time I got there the figure was gone.

"Who was that?" I asked. "Our friend?"

"No, it was a Frankenstein," Frank said. "Or maybe a werewolf. I couldn't tell."

I grinned. Haunted houses usually had a few park workers in them who would dress up as monsters so they could jump out and scare you. I'd always thought that would be a cool job to have.

I heard a hissing sound, and suddenly the room was filled with smoke.

Was this the trap?

I took a shallow breath. It was only fog from a fog machine. I had a hard time seeing Frank through the haze. And if there were any clues in this room, I couldn't see those, either.

"Joe, in here!" Frank called.

His voice was coming from the left. I moved that way. Soon enough, I spotted him to my right. I stopped, confused.

"Frank?"

"Over here." His voice was still coming from the left, but I could see him standing on the right, gesturing to me with his hand.

I walked toward him—and smacked into a wall.

Not a wall. A mirror.

"All right!" I cried happily. "A hall of mirrors!"

"I still haven't seen anything unusual," Frank said from behind me. When I turned around, he was gone.

He appeared again to the left. "What kind of evidence do you think we're looking for?"

I moved left, and hit another mirror. Where was Frank?

When I turned around, I saw a room filled with . . . me. Reflections of myself looked back at me from every direction. "Who knows?" I answered Frank. "I figure we'll recognize it when we see it."

Suddenly a tall man appeared in the mirrors, standing right behind me.

I spun around, freaked out. No one was there.

"Hello?" I called. "Is someone else here?"

A deep, maniacal laugh echoed through the room. But all I could see was myself, everywhere.

"Frank?" I said. "Are you still in here?"

No answer.

"Frank?"

Someone grabbed my arm. I jumped and let out a yell.

It was Frank.

"There's nothing here," he said. "Let's keep going."

The next hallway was pitch black. It had slimy

things hanging from the ceiling and something that felt like cobwebs stretched across the center. I sighed. "These haunted houses are all the same," I complained. "I was hoping for something scarier."

"I was hoping for some evidence," Frank said.

A woman dressed like a vampire appeared and screamed in my face.

I didn't even gasp. I was getting bored.

"Maybe we should try to go backstage, or whatever they call it in haunted houses," I suggested to Frank. "Our friend didn't say the evidence would be part of the attraction. Maybe there's something hidden through that back door we saw yesterday."

"It's worth a try," Frank said, pushing his way past a suit of armor that had suddenly started moving. "Let's get through the rest of this thing, get outside, and circle around the back."

"Okay." A zombie jumped out in front of me.

I waited for it to leave.

It waved its arms and let out a growl.

"Aaahhh," I yelled halfheartedly. Maybe it would move on now.

"Joe, come on," Frank said from the other side of the zombie.

"Uh, excuse me," I told the zombie. I stepped around it.

As I joined Frank on the other side, the zombie roared again.

Then it grabbed my head with one hand.

It grabbed Frank's head with the other hand.

And it smashed our heads together—hard.

12.

ZOMBIE!

My head was killing me. There was a woodpecker sitting on my shoulder and pecking me over and over with its beak. It hurt like crazy, but I couldn't lift my arm to shoo the bird away.

"Frank."

Seriously, I had a splitting headache. I glanced over and saw that it wasn't a woodpecker after all. It was Playback, my parrot. "Zombie!" he squawked. He kept pecking me in the head.

"Frank."

I recognized my brother's voice, but I didn't answer him. My head hurt too much. And Playback wouldn't stop pecking me.

"Frank, wake up."

I'm dreaming, I thought. *Playback isn't pecking me.*

"Frank!"

"I am awake," I muttered. "Leave me alone. My head hurts."

I tried to remember if I had any aspirin nearby. My bedroom is only a few feet from the bathroom, and there would probably be aspirin in the medicine chest. But my head hurt too much. I didn't want to move.

"Frank, open your eyes," Joe commanded. "*Now.*"

I opened my eyes. I waited for the sunlight to hit me and make my headache worse, but instead all I saw was darkness. I blinked.

My eyes adjusted to the dim light.

This wasn't my bedroom. And I wasn't in bed.

I was sitting up. In a hard chair. And my hands were tied behind me.

"What's going on?" I cried. "Where are we?"

"I think we're in a dungeon," Joe's voice said.

Wait a minute. Where was he? I could hear him, but I couldn't see him. I turned my head to look around—and the headache got worse. "My head is killing me," I said.

"Mine too," Joe answered. "That zombie smashed our heads together. Who would expect it to hurt so much?"

"It knocked us out," I guessed. "He must've hit us pretty hard."

"No kidding," Joe's voice said.

"Where are you?" I asked. "I can't see you."

"I'm behind you," he told me. "We're back to back, I think."

"Can you move?"

"Nope," Joe said. "My hands are tied behind the chair. And my legs are tied to the chair legs."

I took a deep breath and forced myself to ignore the pain in my head. I couldn't afford to be out of it right now. I tried to move my legs. No good. They were tied to my chair. I tried to move my arms, and felt the ropes bite into my wrists. Now that I was paying attention, I could hear Joe moving around behind me.

I looked around the dim room. The only light came from a fake window up near the ceiling. The "window" had bars over it, and behind it was a tiny patch of what was supposed to be the sky—a pale, yellowish light that didn't actually illuminate anything.

The rest of the tiny room was painted gray, with walls that were supposed to look like blocks of stone. Rusted old manacles hung from the walls on all sides. One set of them had a skeleton hanging by its wrists. A pile of bones and a skull lay in one corner, and an animatronic rat sat and twitched its whiskers at us.

"So I guess our friend wasn't a friend," I said finally.

"Guess not," Joe said. "We knew it might be a trap."

"We should've been more careful," I said. "We didn't take that zombie seriously enough."

"We have to figure out how to get out of here," Joe said. "I really need to get to some aspirin."

"This looks like part of the haunted house," I said. "If we can get out of this room, we should be able to find our way outside."

"Yeah, but first we have to get free of these ropes," Joe pointed out.

The deep, evil laugh we'd heard earlier reverberated through the room. Was it part of the haunted house outside?

"I hope you're enjoying the Hall of Horror," the deep voice cackled. "You're going to die here!"

"Is he talking to us, or to the whole haunted house?" Joe murmured.

"I'm talking to *you*, Frank and Joe Hardy," the voice answered as if it heard him. "You're going to die!"

"Who are you?" I yelled, even though it hurt my head.

"I'm a zombie!" The voice laughed maniacally again. I didn't see what was so funny.

"Why are you doing this? Let us go," Joe called.

"I've had enough of your meddling," the voice boomed. "You have no right to snoop around here and make trouble."

"*You're* the one making trouble," I replied. "We're just trying to help."

"You've helped yourselves into an early grave!" the voice cried. "I'll teach you a lesson about sticking your nose into other people's business. You're going to become a permanent part of this haunted house!"

"What do you mean?" I asked.

"You're going to stay where you are, tied up, with no food and no water . . . until you die." The voice laughed again, echoing off the walls. It really hurt my head.

"Don't bother calling for help," the voice added. "People will only think it's part of the Hall of Horror experience."

A door creaked as if it were opening. It was hard to tell what was real in this place, and what was just part of the scary attraction. "Hey!" I called. "Don't leave!"

"I hope you enjoy your deaths," the voice replied. "You only get to die once."

And then the door slammed.

"Hello?" I yelled. "Are you there?"

"We're not done talking to you!" Frank called.

No answer.

The zombie was gone. Or at least he wanted us to think so.

"Do you think he's really gone?" Joe whispered.

"I don't know," I whispered back. "It's impossible to tell. Did you recognize his voice?"

"No," Joe said. "I think he was using a voice distorter. It could have been Uncle Bernie, or Big Jim, or anyone."

"Well, I think we can cross Chris Oberlander off the list," I said. "He couldn't pull off something like this. This is an inside job. Whoever is doing this obviously knows his way around the haunted house."

From somewhere outside the room, a scream split the air. It was followed by some of the creepy organ music.

"I can't believe it," I muttered. "This ride is actually open for business with us stuck inside it."

"Well, we have to get unstuck," Joe said. "How do we untie ourselves?"

I hesitated. For all we knew, the zombie was still listening in on our conversation. But we didn't have much of a choice. We had to try to escape.

I forced myself to think, even though it made my head hurt.

"We're back to back, right?" I whispered.

"Yeah."

"So if we get closer together, we should be able to reach each other's hands, right?"

"Right," Joe said. "And then we can untie each other's ropes!"

"We've done this a million times," I said. "No problem."

"Unless the zombie's still here," Joe murmured. "We better move fast."

I couldn't move my feet very well, but I managed to push my toes along the ground enough to shove the chair back an inch or so. It made a loud scraping sound against the floor.

"Quiet!" Joe hissed.

"I don't have many options," I replied. I shoved the chair back another inch. Behind me I heard Joe doing the same.

After five more shoves, I felt my arms bang into Joe's chair. We maneuvered ourselves sideways until our hands were right next to each other.

Now that I had something to concentrate on, my head didn't hurt as much. I focused on the ropes around Joe's wrists. It didn't take me long to figure out that the zombie had used a basic square knot. Once I knew that, I had the ropes undone in a few seconds.

Joe quickly untied his legs. Then he came over to my chair and untied my hands. I took care of the ropes on my legs.

We were free!

13.

In the Dungeon

"Let's get out of here," I said. I stood up and started rubbing my wrists where the ropes had been.

"Not so fast," Frank said. "Sit back down."

"Why?" Didn't his head hurt as much as mine did? I had zero interest in spending any more time in this dungeon.

"We still don't know who that zombie is," Frank pointed out. "Our mission isn't over until we catch him."

I sat back down. "How are we gonna catch him by staying in here?"

Frank tossed some rope at me. "Tie it around your wrists—loosely," he said.

I was beginning to understand his plan. "We pretend we're still tied up?" I asked.

"Yeah. That zombie guy has to come back and check on us, right?"

"I don't know," I said as I formed the rope into two loops, like handcuffs. "He said he was just going to leave us here to die."

"Yeah, but he can't really do that," Frank said. "At least he has to come back to make sure we haven't escaped. And when he comes back, we'll jump him."

I stuck my hands through the rope and put my arms behind the chair. It wasn't comfortable, but it was better now that the ropes weren't cutting off my circulation. Still, I wasn't convinced that Frank's plan would work.

"Last time he didn't come into the room," I said. "If he still doesn't come in, how can we jump him?"

Frank thought about it.

"Maybe if we pretend we're asleep or uncon-scious again, he'll come in," Frank said.

"Why would we be unconscious?"

"From the blow to our heads," Frank suggested. "Or we could just be exhausted with hunger."

"I guess so," I mumbled. "I *am* exhausted with hunger. How long do you think we've been in here?"

"It's hard to tell," Frank said. "It's so dark in here that it feels like the middle of the night, even though it's probably still daylight outside. Wait." He twisted his wrists out of the rope and pressed the backlight button on his watch. "It's about five." Within a few seconds he was back in the rope.

"I hope he comes back soon," I said.

But he didn't. We must've waited at least an hour, pretending we were tied up, listening to the sounds of people screaming and laughing in the halls of the haunted house. Nobody came near the dungeon, though. The zombie must've closed it off somehow.

Finally the screams of people outside stopped. The creepy organ music went away. Everything grew silent.

"It seems like the ride is closed," Frank whispered.

"Could be," I whispered back.

Suddenly we heard footsteps in the hallway outside.

"Play dead," Frank whispered.

I closed my eyes and let my head fall forward onto my chest as if I were deeply asleep, or just passed out.

I heard the jingle of keys, and then a door was opened. I kept my eyes closed as someone entered the dungeon. The footsteps were heavy, and I could hear him breathing.

"Now!" Frank yelled.

I jumped up and shook the fake bonds off my wrists. Frank did the same.

The zombie jumped in surprise, but he didn't back off. Instead he pulled a knife from inside his costume and held it out toward us.

I froze. I hadn't been expecting a weapon. And I figured Frank would be surprised too. We'd been planning to rush the guy, but right now that didn't seem like such a good idea.

The room was so dark that I could barely make out the steel glinting in his hand. With the three of us in there, the place was too small to maneuver. If we tried to run or to fight him, chances were good that one of us would get stabbed.

The zombie laughed. He was going for that same deep, maniacal laugh as before. But he didn't have the voice distorter now—probably he had to use the haunted house PA system to do that.

"You didn't expect me to come armed, did you?" he asked.

He was still disguising his voice, but it wasn't as deep as it had been through the distorter. It sounded familiar . . . but was it Uncle Bernie's voice? Big Jim's? I couldn't tell.

"I decided starvation was too good for you," the zombie went on. "It would take too long, and then I'd have to keep the dungeon closed off." He gave another deep laugh and lunged at me with the knife.

I jumped backward. The knife flashed through the air a few inches from my throat.

"And the dungeon is everybody's favorite part of the Hall of Horror," he continued. "Don't you like it?"

"No," Frank said.

The zombie laughed again. "Too bad. It's the last place you'll ever see."

This time he brandished the knife at Frank. Frank twisted away and jumped over next to me. "We can't keep doing this," I whispered. "The room's too small. He'll hit one of us soon."

"I have a plan," Frank murmured.

But before he could say anything else, the zombie lunged at us with the knife. I couldn't see much in the darkness, so I just spun away from Frank and tried to get behind the dark figure of the zombie.

He'd come through a door—where was it?

I glanced frantically around the room, searching for the way out. But all I saw were the fake stone walls. The door must be hidden in one of the walls.

The zombie gave a roar and lunged forward again. At least the darkness was working against him, too.

"Joe," Frank called.

"Over here," I replied.

"Remember Vijay!" he said.

Huh? My guess was that Frank was trying to let me in on his plan, but I didn't understand what he meant. *Remember Vijay?*

I forced myself to keep calm and think it through, even though the zombie was still two feet away holding a knife on us.

Vijay. Vijay Patel, the guy who'd delivered pizza—and our last mission—to the house? What did I know about Vijay?

He was an ATAC trainee.

He was originally from India.

He thought Frank and I were heroes.

He'd given us a pocket strobe light.

That's it! I thought. *Frank must have the pocket strobe with him.*

Leave it to my brother to be totally prepared at all times. That's why he's such an excellent ATAC agent.

"I remember," I called.

"Now!" Frank yelled.

I closed my eyes. Even through my eyelids I could see the flash of bright blue light as Frank hit the button on the strobe.

The zombie let out a yelp of surprise. He'd been

blinded by the light in the dark room. I listened to where the yell came from so I'd know where he was in the darkness.

"Now!" Frank yelled again.

This time I didn't close my eyes. I was ready for the flash of light. When it came, I had a brief view of the guy in the huge zombie costume as he stumbled backward. The knife in his hand glinted in the blue light.

I kicked it out of his hand.

The knife clattered across the floor.

Frank hit the strobe again. In the light we saw the zombie running toward the wall. I tackled him to the ground. A second later I felt Frank jump on top of him as well.

"Tie his hands," Frank cried, shoving some of the rope toward me.

We wrestled the guy's hands behind his back and tied them together. It wasn't easy in the darkness.

As soon as we had him tied, I decided it was time to let a little light in.

"He was going for the wall over here," I told Frank. "The door must be hidden here somewhere."

Frank flashed the strobe again, and in the split second of bright light I spotted the outline of a door cut into the "stone" wall.

I felt for it in the darkness and managed to find the edge. Feeling downward, I found a tiny latch. I threw the latch and yanked the door open.

Outside, the halls of the haunted house were lit with work lights—the kind they only turn on when the ride is closed.

Compared with the dim light of the dungeon, it seemed like the brightest sunlight I'd ever seen.

"Okay, let's see who this zombie is," Frank muttered.

I helped him push the guy over onto his back, and then I sat on his chest to make sure he stayed down.

Frank pulled off the zombie mask.

I watched anxiously. Was it Big Jim? Uncle Bernie?

"Get off of me," the zombie whined.

I stared in disbelief.

It was Little Bernie.

14.

MISSION ACCOMPLISHED

"I should've known when I saw how tall the zombie was," Joe said, shaking his head.

I shrugged. "I figured that was just the costume."

"You guys are in big trouble," Little Bernie whined.

"Get up," I told him. "*You're* the one in trouble." We dragged him to his feet and led him through the haunted house. He cried the whole way. He was such a big guy it was easy to forget that he was still just a kid.

Joe found a door labeled EMERGENCY EXIT and pushed it open.

I was shocked to see sunlight come streaming in. When we stepped outside, the park was as crowded and bustling as ever.

149

"I thought the park was closed for the night," I said.

"It's only two-thirty," Joe said, checking the big clock over the concert bandstand. "Little Bernie must've just closed the haunted house so he could deal with us."

"What's going on here?" Uncle Bernie demanded. He came storming up to us, three security guards behind him. When he spotted Little Bernie, he gasped. "Son? What are you doing in that costume?"

"He was trying to kill us," I said.

Uncle Bernie's eyebrows shot up. "What? That's impossible." He looked his son up and down. Little Bernie kept crying. "He was probably just working in the haunted house, and he tried to scare you. That's the job of the zombie." Uncle Bernie didn't sound too certain.

"The haunted house was closed, remember?" one of the security guards put in. "That's why we were coming here to check it out."

Uncle Bernie's face fell. "It shouldn't have been closed in the middle of the day," he said. "Why was it, son?"

Little Bernie just sobbed even harder, snot and tears rolling down his face.

"Your son is the one who set off the M-80 on the

roller coaster," I told Uncle Bernie. "He also hooked up a generator to the carousel to make it go too fast. For all we know, he broke the safety bar on the Ferris wheel, too."

"And yesterday he pretended to be poisoned by a hot dog in order to throw us off the trail," Joe put in. "He wanted us to think Big Jim had done it, but we didn't fall for it." He frowned at Little Bernie. "We know you're the one who's been sabotaging the park all along."

"That's impossible," Uncle Bernie said. But he looked scared. "Tell me the truth, Bernie."

"Why did they have to come here?" Little Bernie blubbered. "They ruined everything!"

"Did you have something to do with what happened at the water park yesterday, Bernie?" I asked. "Were you trying to get rid of us then?"

"I know a kid who works there," he sobbed. "I bet him fifty dollars he wouldn't put the cover on the tube. I didn't do it!"

"No, you just paid someone else to do it," Joe said grimly.

"What are you talking about?" Uncle Bernie asked.

"A kid named Marc Krakowski tried to kill us at Splash World yesterday," I explained. "Just like

Little Bernie tried to kill us in the Hall of Horror five minutes ago. And just like he killed Maggie Soto on the Doom Rider last week."

"I didn't mean to!" Little Bernie cried. "I just wanted a little bit of the roof to collapse so people on the roller coaster would be scared. I didn't think a stupid firecracker would make such a big explosion. It was an accident!"

One of the security guards pulled out his walkie-talkie and radioed for the police.

Uncle Bernie had gone pale. "But why, son?" he gasped. "Why would you do such horrible things?"

"I hate this stupid park!" Little Bernie cried. "It's the only thing you care about! You don't care about Mom, or me, or anything. Just the dumb amusement park!"

"That's not true," Uncle Bernie protested.

"Yes, it is," Little Bernie sobbed. "I thought if people got scared to come here, you'd have to close the place down. Then we could have a normal life and you would pay some attention to me."

Uncle Bernie looked as if someone had punched him in the gut. "I only care about the park because I want it to be yours someday," he said. "I never dreamed that you felt this way."

"You never bothered to ask me," Little Bernie spat.

A siren rang through the air, and a cop car came driving slowly through the crowd that had gathered outside the haunted house.

Two police officers got out of the car and walked over to take Little Bernie into custody.

He was still crying as they put him in the backseat of their cruiser.

Uncle Bernie turned to us, still horrified. "I . . . I had no idea," he said again.

"I know," I told him. "I'm sorry about your son."

He blinked at me. "I'm sorry he tried to kill you," he said. "I don't know what to do."

"Your son could use a father right now," Joe said. "Frank and I are fine. We can take care of ourselves."

Uncle Bernie nodded slowly. He turned to watch as the cops closed the door on his son. "Wait," he called suddenly. "Wait for me."

He hurried over and got into the backseat next to Little Bernie.

"Maybe now Little Bernie will get the attention he was looking for," Joe said. He turned to me and smiled. "Another successful mission. We got the perp."

"Yeah," I said. "I never expected it to be a kid."

"Want to hit the log flume before we leave?" Joe asked.

I thought about it. But right now, Uncle Bernie's Fun Park was anything but fun. "Nah," I said. "Let's just go home."

"I have a better idea," Joe said. "Let's go back and find Vijay. We have to tell him how his pocket strobe—and some ATAC training—saved us from a zombie!"